Library of Congress Cataloging in Publication Data

Arthur, Herbert, 1899–1975.
    The black rider.

    Reprint. Originally published: England: Chivers Press: 1962.
    1. Large type books.   I. Title.
[PS3501.R77B57   1985]   813′.52   84–17577
ISBN 0–89340–852–2

British Library Cataloguing in Publication Data

Arthur, Burt
    The black rider.—Large print ed.—
    (Atlantic large print)
    Rn: Herbert Arthur Shappiro   I. Title
    813′.52[F]   PS3501.R77

    ISBN 0-7451-9032-4

This Large Print edition is published by Chivers Press, England, and
John Curley & Associates, Inc, U.S.A. 1985

Published by arrangement with Donald MacCampbell, Inc

U.K. Hardback ISBN 0 7451 9032 4
U.S.A. Softback ISBN 0 89340 852 2

THE BLACK RIDER

Gun Hawk, Law Dog, Bounty Man, Thief—each had a bullet for the Black Rider. He rode the outlaw trail alone with a price on his head and every lawman and bounty hunter in Texas on his heels. He lived by his wits and by his gun and the only law he recognized was Colt justice. Men called him the Black Rider. He rode the outlaw trail alone, till the day when he put his head in a noose—for a woman.

THE BLACK RIDER

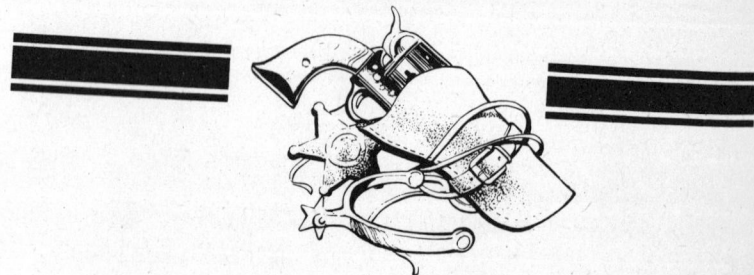

Burt Arthur

ATLANTIC LARGE PRINT
Chivers Press, Bath, England.
John Curley & Associates Inc.,
South Yarmouth, Mass., USA.

THE BLACK RIDER

CHAPTER ONE

On the rolling plains, midway between Cheyenne and the distant, shadowy Black Hills, a train of canvas-topped prairie-schooners had halted for a noon-day meal. There were eight wagons in the train and they were drawn up in a circle. In the center of the circle a fire crackled brightly. It was cheery and comforting, for despite the sun overhead there was a sharp tang in the air fostered by a swift, biting wind that swept southward, over the prairie land.

There was too a savory breath of freshly roasted venison in the crisp air and huge slabs of steaming meat still hung on crude, hastily-fashioned spits above the fire. There were a dozen men grouped around the fire, and, with one exception, they were all rough, bearded and grizzled, with the deep bronze of the great outdoors, the wind and the sun, in their faces.

The exception was a buckskin-clad youth; handsome and dark, tall, lean and supple, with the narrow waist and broad shoulders of an athlete. Straight as an oak he stood, towering some three or four inches over the tallest of his companions. He chewed his meat quietly, glanced at his mates from time to

1

time, listened to their conversation but made no attempt to join in, smiled fleetingly when something one of the men said made the others laugh uproariously.

He had joined the train a few miles out from Cheyenne. He had simply cantered up astride an eye-filling, free-striding blue roan, reined in alongside the train leader and asked permission to join the party. He had given his name as Smith and said he was heading for the hill country; added that if they would take him along he would serve as hunter or guide or in whatever capacity his services might best be used, until his destination was reached.

The train was under command of an irascible old plainsman named Joe Cox. The latter studied the newcomer for a moment, swept him with an appraising eye, then turned slowly and thoughtfully toward the expanse of prairie land ahead. While he did not approve of strangers who simply rode up and barged in, another man who could ride and shoot was always a welcome addition, particularly if the party ran into Indians.

The surrounding country, particularly that which lay ahead, the shadowy woodlands, the soggy treacherous badlands, the difficult and hazardous passes that wound through the rough and hilly country, were fraught with peril. There were, as all plainsmen knew, war-parties of marauding Indians roaming the plains, searching for the inexperienced, the unwary and the defenseless. Massacres were so common that now they had become routine. There were, too, bands of outlaws abroad, hard-riding, fast-shooting white men with prices on their heads; white men who were just as ruthless and wanton as the feared Redmen.

Danger lurked at every turn and at every crossing. The distant clumps of wild bushes, the huge boulders, the great trees, the towering, forbidding canyon walls; all were made to order for ambuscades. One never knew what lay ahead. Unseen foes, both red and white, watched from places of concealment and when the opportunity arose, struck with fury and dispatch. This was the West, the great unknown, a virgin country in the making, a new country in which the forces of nature and evil combined to drive out and wipe out those who sought to forge a path upon which other pioneers might tread. It was a country in which only the hardiest survived; a country in which might made right; a country in which the span of a man's years depended largely upon his skill with the Colt six-gun and Winchester.

Cox had watched Smith as he had loped across the plains. He had noted with an approving eye that Smith rode well; noted too that the brace of six-guns that swung low against his thighs within easy reach of his hands were not there for 'show.' There were unmistakable signs that an experienced hand like Cox quickly recognized; signs that told him at a glance that they were the tools of a craftsman. The dandy chose pearl-handled guns as a general rule. The capable workman chose wooden-handled weapons such as Smith wore. Then, too, the smooth, worn gun butts indicated usage. Cox nodded briefly. Smith wheeled his mount away and clattered down the line and took his place behind the last wagon. Another rider looked up at him, nodded and edged away to make room on the trail for Smith.

It was late afternoon some few days after Smith had joined the train that Cox pulled out of line and beckoned Smith to join him. The youth cantered up and fell in beside Cox. At a word from the leader, they spurred their mounts and galloped off across the plains. They were nearing the Black Hills, the most dangerous spot of all, and wise old Cox wanted to look at the country ahead before ordering the train on. For a while the horsemen rode together, knee to knee, then the big roan began to run. Smith tightened his rein and spoke sharply to his horse. For a

4

minute the roan fought for his head, then he subsided and slackened his pace.

They clattered over rock and shale and followed a trail that led uphill. After they had put a mile between them and the train, Cox reined in and dismounted. He tossed the reins over the horse's head and trudged off toward a knoll that commanded a view of the plains below. For a few minutes he studied the open country, glanced fleetingly at the hills above him, then apparently satisfied that it was safe to continue the westward trek, marched back to his horse and swung himself up into the saddle. Together they wheeled and rode slowly down the trail. Suddenly a muffled scream reached them. They halted as one and looked at each other questioningly. Smith sat upright in his saddle, listening intently. Cox was motionless.

'What was that?'

Cox shrugged his shoulder.

'I dunno.'

'The hell you don't,' Smith said evenly.

Cox's eyes narrowed.

'Mebbe,' he answered quietly, 'only I ain't that curious that I aim to find out.'

He touched his horse's flanks with his spurs and started down the trail again. 'Neither do you, son,' he called over his shoulder. After a minute he halted and turned in his saddle.

Smith sat motionless, still listening.

'Come on, son,' Cox called. 'Time we was gettin' back.'

Smith turned slowly in his saddle. He shook his head.

'I aim to have a look around first, ' he said quietly.

Cox stiffened in his saddle.

'I'm orderin' you back, Smith,' he said harshly. 'Start ridin'.'

Smith grinned boyishly.

'Sure,' he answered lightly, then nodding up the trail. 'I'm ridin' that way.'

He wheeled his horse and clattered up the trail. Cox stared after him for a moment, shook his head angrily, and muttered something to himself.

'Yuh damn fool!' he yelled.

He jabbed his spurs into the horse's flanks and rode off to meet the train.

The roan, given his head, raced up the incline. When they reached the top of the trail and broke onto level ground, Smith reined in and looked about. Dusk was upon him now and in the gathering darkness the jagged Black Hills seemed strangely silent, almost forbidding. The roan pawed nervously and Smith checked him and held him still. He turned and looked down the trail. There was no sign of Cox. All he could see was a long

6

slope dotted with groves and thickets through which the trail wound. His eyes narrowed and he loosened the right hand Colt in its swinging holster.

'Just in case,' he heard himself say.

A rifle cracked close by and a bullet whined and sped overhead. Smith slid out of the saddle hastily. His guns were in his hands by the time his booted feet touched the ground. The roan needed no command to move. He wheeled and dashed away. There was some thick underbrush close at hand and Smith dove into it cursing at the sharp briars that tore at his face and clothes. When the second shot rang out, Smith was ready. He spied the flashes of gunfire and his heavy Colts roared in answer. There was a dull thud close by, the sound of a falling body. Smith scrambled to his feet and plunged forward toward the spot.

He stumbled over a log and cursed softly, then he halted and looked down at it. It was the body of a man that lay at his feet and Smith bent over him. The man was dead, his face a battered bloody smear, a tribute to his marksmanship and to the effectiveness of the Colts. The man's rifle lay a few feet away and Smith picked it up. The barrel was still hot. There was a tiny clearing just beyond and Smith pushed his way through the brush and stared hard at what he saw.

7

The figure of a woman sagged against a post to which she was tied. There was angry welts across her bared back, the tell-tale welts of a whip. The woman groaned softly. Smith shoved his guns into their holsters, dropped the rifle and bounded forward. A minute later he lowered his unconscious burden to the ground. There were some torn garments near by and he managed to get her arms into the sleeves of one of them, buttoned it rather clumsily across her breasts. He straightened up and whistled shrilly. Soon he heard the roan's answering neigh. He whistled a second and third time to guide the horse, then the roan trotted up, Smith went forward to meet him, rubbed the roan's nose and reached for his canteen that hung from the saddle-horn. He was glad that he had refilled the canteen that very day. He bent over the woman again, pillowed her head in the hollow of his arm and forced some of the water through her parched lips. Presently, she stirred and moaned again. He caught up another of her garments, something white and lacey, soaked it with water and swabbed her face and wrists with it. The cold water seemed to revive her for she opened her eyes slowly and stared hard at him. Then her eyes closed again, gently, and she slipped away into unconsciousness.

For a moment he considered moving her.

The dead man might have companions and they might return. Then he decided that he would have to chance it. It would be difficult moving the woman, a dead burden in the darkness. Smith lowered her to the ground again, covered her with one of the blankets from his roll. For a moment he stood over her, rubbing his chin reflectively. This, he told himself, was a fine situation. At his feet lay an unconscious woman, while a short distance away lay the body of a dead man, a man he'd never seen before yet who had tried to shoot him. All he needed now to fill his cup to overflowing was a band of rampaging Indians.

Smith tethered the roan close by, reloaded his Colts, draped the second blanket from his saddle roll over his shoulders and squatted down, cross-legged, beside the motionless form of the woman. He glanced at her and thought she was breathing quite normally now. By morning he guessed she'd be all right again. He wondered what connection there was between her and the dead man who lay in the thicket beyond. He wondered, too, who she was and what she was like. He was sure that in the morning light she'd turn out to be a prairie wife, faded and worn. He drew the blanket closer. It was chilly now and a strong, biting wind swept down over him. He knew that he would be colder as the long night wore on. He laid the rifle he had picked up across his knees, sighed and pictured the men in the wagon train, grouped around the crackling camp fire, eating their fill of freshly-roasted venison. He shook his head; presently he closed his eyes.

It was dawn when he awoke and a bright, warm sun beat down upon him. He was chilled and stiff and he cursed softly; he turned and glanced at the blanketed woman. He blinked and stared hard at her. The prettiest girl he had ever seen lay on her side, looking up at him.

CHAPTER TWO

It was midnight and Deadwood City lay basking in a flood of yellow moonlight that cast long shadows from the pine forests of the surrounding mountain peaks, and glinted upon the swift, swirling, muddy waters of Whitewood Creek which swept past the town on its journey southward.

A horseman riding north through Custer Gulch, halted on the edge of town, wheeled his horse out of the stage road and piloted him toward a tree upon which someone had nailed a placard. For a few minutes he leaned forward in his saddle, traced each word slowly in the dim light, then he sat back and laughed. He ripped the placard from the tree, folded it and shoved it into his shirt. Then he whirled his horse and cantered on into town.

Deadwood's only street ran north and south through the town. Rows of wooden lean-tos and larger buildings lined both sides of the narrow, muddy street. The horseman reined in and surveyed the scene before him. He was amazed at Deadwood's crowds and at their activity. The town's few stores and many saloons were alive with customers and ablaze with light.

Other men rode by, glanced at him fleetingly as they passed. Some of them, however, turned in their saddles and looked back at him. His black horse, black costume, even his black gloves gave him a sinister appearance that blended with the night. Now, in the yellow moonlight he seemed a spectre horseman. He nudged his horse with his knees and the horse moved on slowly up the street.

There were shouts from the saloons. Now two men suddenly stepped into the street, squared off and proceeded to maul each other. Passersby merely glanced at them but made no attempt to halt or interfere with them. Presently a third man stepped out of a saloon, strode over to the combatants and separated them, then he led them back into the saloon.

Now a shot rang out and a man staggered out of the saloon, stumbled into the street and pitched forward on his face in the mud. It was the man who had acted as peacemaker. Two men came dashing out, smoking guns in their hands, vaulted into the saddles of their horses sidling in front of the saloon and raced down the street. They turned the corner as other men poured into the street. Some of the men fired after the disappearing horsemen, then they holstered their guns and went back inside. The black rider recognized the two men as the street fighters.

There was a third horse standing at the rail in front of the saloon and now he backed away, trotted toward the motionless man lying in the street, halted beside him and nudged him. The fallen man failed to respond. The horse raised his head high and neighed. Other men crossing the street looked over but continued on their way.

The black rider halted in front of the saloon too. He dismounted and dropped the reins over his horse's head, patted the horse's flank and marched across the wooden planking that served as a walk and strode into the saloon. In the doorway he halted for a moment. The place was crowded and it reeked from smoke and ale. He dropped a coin upon the bar. The bartender, a lean, cadaverous individual, nodded, slid a bottle across the surface of the bar and followed it with a glass. Another man entered, halted in the doorway too, and glanced around the room. He was a big man, burly and heavier than the black rider. The latter glanced at him sideways and noted that the newcomer wore a silver star on his shirt. The big man nodded to the bartender, glanced at the black rider and stepped up to him.

'Howdy,' he said briefly. His voice was deep and harsh.

'Howdy,' came the answer.

'Stranger here?'

'You got good eyes, Mister.'

The sheriff flushed slightly.

'Where you from?'

'Home.'

'Where you headin'?'

'Other places.'

The flush deepened on the sheriff's face. Anger flared up into his eyes.

'I'm sheriff o' this county, stranger,' he said coldly.

'So what?'

'When I ask questions around these parts I expect answers,' the sheriff concluded.

The black rider smiled fleetingly.

'It's my bet you're a heap better at questions than at answers,' he said lightly.

13

The sheriff's hand dropped to the butt of the heavy Smith & Wesson that sagged his hip. Every muscle of his body was tense and rigid. The black rider kept his hands on the bar. The sheriff's hand fell away from his gun butt.

'I'll be seein' you again, stranger,' he said significantly.

'I aim to see you again, too, sheriff,' the black rider answered.

The sheriff turned slowly and headed for the door. A man entered, collided with the sheriff who shouldered him out of the way, then he strode out. The man stared after him for a moment, then he shrugged his shoulder and sauntered away toward the rear of the saloon. The bartender wiped the bar in front of the black rider, then he leaned over the bar.

''Pears to me I've seen you some place, stranger,' he began slowly.

He straightened up and wiped the bar again. After a minute he stopped, raised his eyes.

'What might your name be, stranger?'

'You askin' for any special reason?'

The bartender shook his head.

'Nope. Guess I'm jest a mite curious. That's all.'

The black rider smiled fleetingly.

'Curious, eh? Now me, well, I'm different,

14

see? My trouble is rememberin' things.'

The bartender seemed a bit puzzled at this ailment.

'What kinda things, stranger?'

The black rider leaned over the bar, beckoned to the bartender to come a bit closer. The latter, however, drew back and eyed the black rider suspiciously.

'Oh, names 'specially. Funny, ain't it?'

The bartender frowned.

'Mebbe,' he said.

The black rider lowered his voice.

'Right now, pard, I ain't sure if my name's Jones or Brown or McGillicuddy. Why, I might even be that feller Marshall, you know, the hombre the law's so anxious to catch up with. See?'

The bartender didn't see right off. Instead he studied the black rider for a moment, then he nodded slowly.

'Yep,' he said, nodding as he spoke, 'you might be, mightn't you?' Then he shook his head vigorously. 'Naw, you couldn't be. This Marshall hombre is plain mean and ornery. Gotta be to put killin' and bank robbin' on a payin' basis, y'know, Mister.'

The black rider shrugged his shoulder. He reached for the bottle, poured himself a drink, drained the glass and set it down upon the bar. There was a strange and curious look of

15

mingled doubt and wonder on the bartender's face. The black rider winked at him and strolled off. The bartender rubbed his bristly chin reflectively, mumbled something under his breath and wiped the bar again, vigorously. He stopped once and looked over at the black rider, shook his head and continued wiping.

The black rider halted at the faro table, watched the play for a minute, then he continued around the crowded room. Presently he halted again at a corner table at which two men were seated playing cards. One of the men, an overdressed, professional gambler, looked up at him and scowled. The second man, a good-looking, well-dressed man in his early thirties, looked up too and nodded pleasantly. There was an unoccupied chair at the table and the black rider swung it around and seated himself. The gambler eyed him sharply.

'Sittin' in, Mister?'

'Nope. Jest watchin'. I get a kick outta watchin' sleeves,' he answered significantly.

His hand streaked to his gun. It flashed in his hand. He fanned it for a moment and shoved it back into his holster. The gambler opened his mouth as if to speak, thought better of it after the display of gun dexterity and closed his mouth grimly. The game went

16

on. The gambler lost five hands in rapid succession. His opponent grinned broadly.

'Doin' all right, eh, Mister?' the black rider asked.

The man nodded and grinned again. The black rider got to his feet slowly, turned away, halted and retraced his steps. Then he leaned over the table.

'If your luck changes sudden-like, Mister,' he said quietly, 'you might look up this gent's sleeve.'

The gambler flushed. He cursed, pushed his chair away from the table, his ring hand streaking toward a shoulder-holster under his coat. The black rider caught the gambler's wrist with his own left hand, then his right fist thudded cruelly against the man's jaw. Man and chair went over backwards. A heavy Colt gleamed in the black rider's hand. He stepped around the table, kicked the chair out of his way and bent over the gambler.

'Get up,' he commanded.

The gambler shook his muddled head. A iron hand shot out, gripped his coat front and yanked him to his feet. Men crowded around but the black rider paid no attention to them.

'Next time you go for your gun, Mister,' he said coldly, 'be sure it's loose in your holster.'

He dragged the dazed gambler back to the table.

'You lose any money to this gent, Mister?' the black rider asked the second man.

The man counted the bills and coins on the table in front of him. Presently he looked up.

'About forty dollars,' he answered briefly.

'Hand it over,' he commanded.

The gambler hesitated for a moment, but his eyes faltered. He dug into his pocket, produced a roll of bills, counted out forty dollars and dropped the money on the table. The black rider shoved the money across the table, nodded to the second man who picked it up and put it in his pocket. The black rider turned again to the gambler, caught his right wrist and with a quick motion ripped open the man's sleeve. Four cards, among them three aces, fluttered to the floor. He laughed and shoved the gambler away. A murmur arose, then a babble of excited voices hummed throughout the packed saloon.

The gambler backed away toward the wall. Fury showed in his face. He turned for a moment, evidently looked for someone, spied two men idling at the bar and nodded to them vigorously. They nodded understandingly in reply. They whipped out their guns. The gambler tore open his coat and a Colt gleamed in his hand.

The bartender who had witnessed the proceedings, suddenly leaned over the bar and

18

struck one of the men over the head with a bungstarter. There was a dull, sickening thud. The bartender dived under the bar. The man dropped his gun and fell like a poled steer. The black rider whirled like a cat. The second man at the bar and the gambler fired at him simultaneously. The black rider fired from his hips. Flame belched from the muzzles of his guns and smoke swirled about him. The roar of the shots filled the saloon. The second gunman staggered away from the bar, swayed and crashed full length to the floor.

Some few feet away, the gambler dropped his gun, clutched at his chest, fell against a table and slid to the floor. For a moment his left leg twitched, then he lay still. Smoke curled ceilingward from the black rider's guns. His eyes swept the saloon. A cold, mocking smile toyed at the corners of his mouth.

'Anybody else aimin' to take a hand in this?' he asked.

There was no answer; merely a shuffling of feet. He shoved the Colts into their holsters and turned to the man at the table.

'Reckon it's past your bedtime, Mister,' he drawled.

The man nodded and got to his feet. The black rider followed him to the door.

'Git on your horse, Mister,' he said in a low

19

tone, 'and don't stop for nuthin'.'

The man made no reply. He simply strode out. The black rider strolled back to the bar. The usual bottle and glass slid forward. He poured himself a drink. The bartender edged over and pretended to be busy wiping the bar. The black rider sensed that he wanted to tell him something. He raised his glass slowly to his lips.

'Watch your step leavin', Mister,' he heard the bartender say in a low tone. 'Couple o' that card palmer's friends might be waitin' outside.'

The black rider nodded, drained his glass and set it down. He tossed a coin on the bar and turned toward the door. The bartender straightened up.

'Hey, Mister,' he called.

The black rider halted and looked back.

'Yeah?'

'Recollect what your name was?' the bartender asked.

The black rider rubbed his chin with the back of his hand for a moment, thoughtfully, shook his head and laughed lightly, sheepishly.

'Shucks, yes, pardner,' he answered shortly. 'But, doggone it, if I ain't plumb forgot it again. Don't that beat all?'

The bartender frowned. The black rider

20

turned again, loosened the Colts in their holsters and stepped outside. For a moment he was motionless, save for his hands which slid mechanically towards the butts of the Colts. He took a single step forward. A rifle cracked and a bullet whined over his head and plowed into the framework above the door. He ducked instinctively. One of his Colts answered, then he dashed across the wooden planking, vaulted into the saddle and wheeled his horse away from the rail.

In a darkened doorway opposite the saloon a shadowy figure edged out and fired at him. Two other figures took shape in the doorway too. The black rider, bent low over his horse's neck, fired back. The shadowy figure stumbled and fell. The other two figures hurdled him and dashed into the street. Their horses waited close by. They raced toward them but before they vaulted into the saddles, the big black horse thundered down the street, swept around the corner and disappeared. A minute later the other two horsemen galloped after him.

The bartender appeared in the doorway and looked out cautiously. He spied the prone figure across the street and stared hard.

''Taint him,' he said shortly, half aloud.

He turned slowly and went back to the bar. He halted and stared down at the limp figure

21

lying there, raised his head and looked over at the sprawled body of the gambler, some distance away.

'Hey,' he yelled. 'Some o' you fellers tote them hombres outta here, willya? Chuck Bartlett, over at the livery stable, will take care o' them.'

Mumbling to himself he stepped behind the bar. He picked up the towel and proceeded to wipe the bar again. He paused and shook his head.

'Reckon I coulda liked that feller,' he said half-aloud. 'But, hell, I wouldn'ta knowed what t' call him. Cain't keep callin' a feller "Hey, Mister" or even "Hey, You." No sir.'

He turned the towel over, and went on wiping the bar.

CHAPTER THREE

Smith stared hard at the girl, stared because he had never seen a face like hers before. He knew he had never seen such blue eyes before; two shining pools of brilliant blue, so full, so soft and tender. He knew, however, that somewhere and sometime he had seen lips like hers before and he recalled that it had been a painting that he had seen. Of course, he had

22

seen pretty girls, girls whose chief claim to beauty lay in their hair. But this girl, well, she wasn't simply attractive because she had blonde or flaxen hair. Those were too commonplace for her. Her hair was golden, just like the sun when it slipped over the jagged Black Hills at dusk. Manlike, he forgot her ills and lost himself in adoration. Womanlike, she too forgot her pains for the moment, forgot them because she was aware that the bronzed youth was carried away by her beauty. Pain, after all, was only secondary to adoration, and she lost herself and all earthly feeling to bask in his admiration. Finally, however, he came back to earth and grinned boyishly.

'Gosh, Ma'm,' he managed to say, 'you're sure pretty.' There was reverence, almost a trace of awe, too, in his voice.

She smiled wanly.

'Thank you, and I suppose I ought to thank you too for saving my life,' he heard her say.

His eyes fell before hers. He tried to laugh to cover his embarrassment, but his laugh was hollow and feeble.

'Shucks, Ma'm,' he answered, 'it wasn't much.' Then he flushed and quickly added, 'I mean I'm glad, Ma'm, that I happened to be passin' when you screamed.' He eyed her questioningly. 'Feelin' more like yourself now?' he asked.

She shook her head slowly.

'I really don't know what I feel like,' she replied. 'After last night . . .' her voice trailed away to nothingness. Evidently she could not erase from her mind the memory of her harrowing experience.

For a moment he thought he saw her chin quiver. He tossed the blanket aside and sprang to his feet. He didn't want her to cry; didn't feel equal to comforting a crying girl.

'You don't have to worry none now,' he said reassuringly. 'The skunk that done it cashed in.'

The girl looked up quickly.

'You mean . . .?'

Smith nodded grimly.

'He's dead as he'll ever be, Ma'm. He's over yonder,' he added, nodding toward the thicket in which the man lay. 'Like to see the coyote?'

A shudder ran through her.

'No,' she said quickly, then bitterly, 'I wish I had never seen him.'

He tried to think of something to say, to add to what she had just said, but nothing came to him, so he simply nodded again. He glanced upward at the sun then turned to her again.

'Reckon you could do with some grub,

Ma'am,' he said, trying to turn her thoughts away from the man who lay in the thicket. He looked down at her almost eagerly. His even teeth shone in his bronzed face.

'Yes, thank you, I suppose I could,' she answered shortly.

She cast the blankets aside and tried to get up. She winced, caught her lips between her teeth, and sank back. He bent over her quickly.

'Gosh, Ma'm,' he said, 'you hadn't ought to do that. You jest stay put. Reckon I can scare up enough grub for this outfit.' He grinned again. 'Course it won't be anythin' fancy, y'understand, jest some flap jacks and coffee.'

His anxiety and his eagerness to serve her touched her. It brought a warm, heartening smile to her face.

'I'm sure I'll find them the best I've ever tasted,' she said lightly.

He laughed and turned away.

'Never can get my flap jacks to stay in one piece,' he said over his shoulder. 'Mebbe when they know we got company they'll sorta behave.'

She heard him stride away through the grass, heard his voice and heard the roan's answering neigh. She turned to look when she heard his step. He had swung his saddle bags over his shoulders. His hands were filled with a varied assortment of pots and pans. He put them down and proceeded to make a fire. She dropped back against the blanket again and looked up at the blue sky. When she heard him come to her side again, she looked up at him. There was a small pan in his hand and under his arm was a white cloth. He placed the pan beside her on the ground and handed her the cloth.

'Jest some water, Ma'm,' she heard him say. 'That there is the back of my shirt. Never did like the blamed thing anyway.'

He turned away again and then halted and retraced his steps and bent over her.

'Reckon I'd better lend a hand here,' he said briefly. He slid his big hands under her arms and lifted her gently into a sitting position. 'That better?'

She smiled up at him.

'Lots better, thanks. But you mustn't baby me, you know,' she scolded.

'No, Ma'am.' Then as an afterthought. 'We'd better do something about that back, Ma'm,' he said shortly. 'Reckon it must hurt a powerful lot.'

He straightened up, hands on his hips, and watched for a moment as she dipped the cloth into the water.

'Breakfast'll be ready right soon,' he said presently. Then, satisfied that she didn't need his help, went back to the fire.

She had finished washing when he returned with a second piece of cloth which he handed her.

'Towel, Ma'm,' he said with a grin.

She returned it to him when she had finished with it. He took it and slung it over his shoulder.

'My hair must be a mess,' she said sadly.

He cocked his head and studied her for a moment.

'Sure is the most beautiful mess I ever did see,' he said gallantly.

He placed a tin plate beside her on the ground and followed it with a whittled stick with two short prongs.

'Plumb outta silverware, Ma'm,' she heard him say. 'Don't look much like a real fork but it's the best we got. I reckon it'll do, though.'

He made another trip back to the fire. It was ten minutes before he returned but when he did, he filled her plate with flap jacks and placed a tin cup of coffee within her reach.

'H'm,' she said brightly. 'Don't they smell good!'

'Better wait 'till you've tasted 'em,' he answered.

He brought his own plate and coffee and squatted down, cross-legged, beside her. When her plate was cleaned, he took it away

27

and brought her another helping.

'H'm, but they're good!'

'Then it's the first time, Ma'm.'

She laughed lightly.

'You're much too modest, Mister . . . ?'

'Jest call me Smith,' he said gravely.

Her blue eyes twinkled.

'John Smith?'

'No, Ma'm, jest plain Smith.'

'But you must have another name, you know,' she said. 'What is it?'

He looked away for a moment. She eyed him curiously, surprised, thought she detected a cloud, a sudden harshness sweep his face. He climbed to his feet presently.

'More coffee, Ma'm?' he asked.

'No, thank you,' she answered.

He picked up her cup and plate and turned away.

'I'm sorry,' she said quietly.

He halted and faced her again.

'Sorry, Ma'm?'

'I've said or asked something that I shouldn't have, haven't I?' she asked, her eyes searching his face.

His eyes were steady and clear. They were gray and she liked them, liked his boyishness, too.

'No, Ma'm.'

'You're just being gallant even though I've

28

been very rude,' he heard her say. 'If you aren't angry with me, then why haven't you asked me my name and something about myself?'

He shrugged his shoulders.

'Reckon I've been waitin' for you to tell me, Ma'm,' he said simply, then with a fleeting smile, 'Your business is, well, your own.'

She pretended to be angry with him, but soon a smile spread over her face. A dimple showed in her cheek. He hadn't noticed it before. He'd have to pay closer attention in the future.

'Oh, I forgot the creed of the West. "Ask no questions".'

He grinned, almost sheepishly.

'Does seem kinda silly, Ma'm.'

'It does not,' she said severely. 'I like the idea behind it. Anyway, I'm Carol Hall.'

'Yes'm.'

'I live about twenty miles from here,' she began. 'My father, Fred Hall, struck gold some months ago. I was away at college, in the East, at the time. Dad was taken ill shortly after and when I arrived here, he ... he was dead.'

'That musta been mighty hard on you, Ma'm, a girl,' he said.

She looked away for a moment.

'Dad hadn't filed his claim. There must

have been some good reason for it. However, I haven't been able to find out what it was. He did send me a map, though. Four men hounded me for it.'

'An' you gave it to 'em?'

'No,' she answered shortly, 'I didn't. They threatened me with all sorts of things and finally, yesterday, they overpowered me and brought me out here.'

'An' forced you to give 'em the map then?' he asked.

She smiled and shook her head.

'Not exactly. I hid the map in my boot. The map they finally found was one I'd copied out of a book,' she explained.

'Good for you, Ma'm,' he said.

'I didn't make it too easy for them to find the second map. I was afraid to, for fear that they'd become suspicious. They were terribly angry at first when I wouldn't tell them where the thing was. They ripped off my blouse and coat, tied me to that post and whipped me. They said they'd leave me here for the vultures.'

His eyes narrowed.

'The hellions,' he muttered between his teeth. 'Go on,' he commanded.

'Then one of the men found the second map. He wanted to untie me, but the leader, he was pretty shrewd, you know, wouldn't let him. He said the map looked kind of funny to him. He took two of the men with him to check up on the map and left the fourth man here to guard me,' she concluded.

'Then they'll be coming back?'

'Yes.'

He was quiet for a moment, then he tossed the plate and cup in the direction of the fire.

'Reckon I'd better get these things together,' she heard him say.

He helped her to her feet, then gathered together the blankets and returned them to the roll behind the saddle. The pots and pans went into the spacious saddle bags. He stamped out the fire, then he picked up the dead man's rifle and carried it away toward a distant boulder. He yanked his own rifle out of its sheath on the saddle and placed it beside the first one. He handed her one of his Colts.

'Reckon you can find a place for that, Ma'm.'

She opened her coat. There was a deep pocket in the thick fleece lining. She dropped the gun into the pocket and looked up at him. He nodded, bent swiftly and swept her up into his arms and carried her through the brush. He halted momentarily for just ahead lay the body of the man he had killed.

'Reckon you'd better cover your eyes, Ma'm,' he said briefly.

31

She turned her head and buried her face in his neckerchief. There was a breath of perfume in her hair and he took a deep breath as he went on again. The roan raised his head when he heard them, turned toward them and neighed. Smith slipped her foot into the stirrup and lifted her into the saddle. He handed her the reins.

'He's gentle as a kitten, Ma'm,' he began. 'Now jest foller the trail down, then swing left, past that big tree yonder and keep goin' till you hit Deadwood.'

She looked at him questioningly. It was evident that she didn't understand him sending her off like this alone.

'I'll hunt you up, Ma'm,' he went on, 'soon's I get to town.'

She looked hard at him again.

'You mean you're staying here?' she asked. There was incredulity in her voice.

He nodded briefly.

'I'm kinda anxious to meet up with those hombres,' he said shortly.

Her eyes flashed.

'I won't go,' she said determinedly.

'Please, Ma'm, there cain't be much time left, y'know,' he said.

She shook her golden head defiantly.

'I don't care. I won't go.'

He looked up at her, his steady gray eyes

32

looking into hers. For a moment their eyes clashed, then a smile spread over his mouth.

'You're a fool, Smith,' she said.

'Yes'm,' he said very gravely.

He took the bridle and led the horse to the edge of the slope.

'Good bye, Ma'm,' he said simply. He swept off his hat and stepped back.

'Smith,' she said.

'Yes'm?'

'Come here, please.'

He stepped forward again, his face turned up to hers. She bent swiftly and kissed him. The roan started off. At that moment a rifle cracked far down below. Smith dashed forward, caught the bridle and swung the roan about.

'Reckon they've come back, Ma'm,' he panted. 'That shot's prob'ly a signal to the other feller. Ride back to that boulder. Turn the horse loose. Then get down behind that boulder and stay there.'

He whacked the roan across the back with his open hand. The horse reared and bounded forward. The girl clung to the reins desperately. She spied an opening in the thicket and piloted him through. When she reached the boulder, she reined in and slid out of the saddle.

'Go, Boy,' she cried.

The roan clattered away. Smith came racing back to her side. She tore open her coat, drew out the Colt and handed it to him. He shoved it into the holster, then he montioned her to get down. She heard the clatter of hoofs, heard the ring of iron on stone and shale, then she heard the voices that grew louder as they came up the trail. She heard a cry, evidence that one of the men had stumbled across the body of the dead man. Her heart pounded and something gripped her and held her tight.

'Easy, Ma'm,' she heard Smith whisper to her, then he stepped past her. She turned quickly, saw him step out, his guns in his hands. 'Reach for the sky, you polecats,' she heard him cry.

For a fleeting second there was silence; a strange, drawn out, ominous silence, then a clap of thunder broke the calm. A roar of pistol shots echoed through the hills. Suddenly she felt no fear; instead she was calm, unexplainably calm. She found herself staring down at two rifles that lay but a few feet away. She recalled that Smith had dropped them there before hoisting her onto the roan. She bent swiftly, picked up one of the rifles and stepped into the open.

She caught a glimpse of the tall, bronzed youth, pistol smoke swirling around him. A huddled form lay but a few feet away from

34

him. She saw the blurred figures of two men plunging forward, two burly men with pistols in their hands. Unconsciously she raised the rifle. When she moved her finger, the rifle seemed to erupt. Through the haze of smoke she saw one of the men, the one nearest her, come to a sudden halt, saw him stagger for a moment, saw his gun drop harmlessly from his numbed fingers, then he plunged forward on his face, his outflung hands grazing her as he fell. She stared down at him. Slowly she put down the rifle.

Now there was no noise, no roar of pistol shots, no clap of thunder, no echoing through the hills. There was no sound, nothing but a heavy, oppressive silence that always follows noise. She felt faint and put out her hand, searching without seeing for something to lean on. She felt herself slipping away and everything faded away into nothingness. She fell to her knees, swayed a bit unsteadily, and slid down to the hard earth. Once she stirred, then she was motionless. Far away a horse whinnied, but only for a moment. Then everything was still.

CHAPTER FOUR

The big black horse thundered along the stage
road. From time to time his rider turned in his
saddle and looked back. He knew that he was
being pursued. Presently the clatter of
pounding hoofs reached him and grew louder.
He laughed and slowed the big black a bit,
whipped out one of his Colts and idled along.
Two mounted figures swung around a bend in
the road and came into full view. The black
rider snapped a quick shot. Two shots came
his way in reply. The heavy Colt roared again,
spitefully, twice, three times. One of the
onrushing horses stumbled and fell, pitching
his rider over his head. The second man fired
twice at the shadowy figure up ahead of him,
reined in his horse, wheeled and cantered
back to where his companion lay. He
dismounted and bent over him. He heard the
big black gallop off, then the clatter of hoofs
died away in the night.

It was shortly after that the black rider
heard the hoof beats of a horse up ahead. He
sent the big black bounding forward again,
overtook the horseman and pulled alongside.
He recognized the man and chuckled.

'Hey, Mister,' he called. 'You still around?'

'Sure,' came the answer.

'Watcha waitin' for?'

'Oh, I figured you'd show up sooner or later,' the man said simply, 'so I just loafed along. What detained you?'

The black rider chuckled.

'Couple o' fellers,' he said shortly.

'I see. By the way, I thought I heard some shooting back there. Did you hear it, too?'

'Shootin'? Now that you mention it, Mister, I reckon I did.'

They jogged along in silence for a few minutes, then the black rider turned to his companion again.

'What's your name, Mister?'

'Redburn.'

'Where you headed for?'

'Oh, nowhere in particular. Why?'

'Jest bein' curious, I reckon.'

'That all? What's your name?'

The black rider chuckled.

'Say, this bein' curious is kinda catchy, ain't it?' he asked.

Redburn laughed lightly.

'Oh, I don't know. I'd like to know because I'm rather indebted to you,' he said shortly.

'Indebted? Forget it, Mister.'

'Hardly. I don't forget things like that in a hurry.'

'You one o' them lawyer fellers, Mister?'

'No,' Redburn answered. 'I'm an engineer, a mining engineer. At least, that's what I've been trained for.'

'That so?'

'Oh, yes. I have a diploma that says so. Remind me to show it to you sometime. By the way, what did you say your name was?'

'I ain't said.'

'Come to think of it, I don't believe you did say, either.'

The black rider laughed.

'Name's Harris,' he said briefly.

'Harris, eh?'

'You don't like the name, mebbe?'

'Oh, one name's as good as another, I suppose,' Redburn answered.

'Meanin' what?'

'Well, to tell the truth, I was just wondering why you discarded Marshall in favor of Harris,' Redburn said quietly.

The black rider was silent for a moment.

'Accusin' a man o' bein' someone else, Mister,' he said quietly, 'is bad business.'

'Ordinarily, yes.'

'Whatever gave you the idea that I ain't the feller I say I am?' the black rider asked.

'Do you know what time it is?' Redburn asked suddenly.

'Nope,' the black rider answered then, 'What's the time got to do with my name,

38

Mister?'

'Just this. Do you own a watch?'

'Supposin' I do?'

'Well, if you do own one, let's see it,' Redburn said.

The black rider chuckled.

'Doggone it, pardner, but I jest remembered leavin' it home on the pianny,' he said lightly.

'I expected something like that. Well, we'll forget about the watch for the present,' he said quietly. 'However, I'd still like to get it back. It means a lot to me. Sentimental reasons, you know.'

'Outside o' bein' some other galoot,' the black rider said presently, 'and stealing your watch, what else are you accusin' me of Mister?'

'Well, I could mention a bank you robbed,' Redburn said quietly. 'It was in Red Dog and I was among those present when you held it up. I know who you are.'

'Why, you . . .'

'Take it easy, Marshall. And don't go for that gun, either,' Redburn said. 'I'm no lawman and I don't intend to hand you over to the law. I thought I recognized you the minute I clapped eyes on you. Now I'm sure of it.'

'Go on.'

'You did me a service tonight,' Redburn

39

continued, 'so we're quits. That is, of course, after you return the watch you ... er ... let us say, borrowed from me.'

The big black horse raised his head and neighed. His rider swung around in his saddle and stared into the darkness. Redburn turned too but he could see nothing for his head. His rider, however, kept his grip on the bridle and held him in check.

'What is it?' Redburn asked.

'Dunno, Mister,' the black rider answered briefly. 'Jest be still a minute.'

They sat in silence for a minute, then both heard the rhythmic beat of running horses' hoofs. Even Redburn could tell that the clatter of iron on stone was that of a large party. He looked at Marshall, questioningly. The black rider jabbed his spurs into his horse's flanks. The big black bounded forward.

'Ride, Mister,' the black rider called over his shoulder. 'Ride like hell!'

Redburn needed no urging. Already he sensed that something was amiss. He spurred his horse and followed hard behind Marshall. When the latter swung off the road and dashed across the prairie land, Redburn followed suit. The roar of hoofs behind them grew louder, then they heard shouts, finally shots. Just who their pursuers were, Redburn couldn't quite figure out. The excitement of the chase made him forget that in the darkness he might be mistaken and shot down despite the fact that he was completely innocent of whatever it might be that the pursuers held against Marshall. It was so dark too, that he marveled at the ability and sure-footedness of the horses to maintain their neck-breaking pace and equilibrium over such rough terrain.

He clung doggedly to the big black's heels for he knew that his only chance of reaching safety depended upon Marshall and upon his own ability to keep up with him. He lashed his horse and drove him on at top speed. He was thankful that Marshall did not urge his own mount on any faster for he knew that if it became necessary, the big black could outrun his horse without difficulty. He bent low over his plunging horse's neck. He kept his eyes fixed on Marshall, not daring to turn for even a moment to look behind.

Shots whined overhead but not within range of them. Marshall slowed his horse just long enough for Redburn to pull alongside.

'What is this all about?' Redburn called.

'Dunno, Mister,' Marshall yelled back.

'Who are those men?' Redburn asked.

'Must be that doggone sheriff and his posse,' Marshall answered over the clatter of hoofs.

'What do they want?'

41

'I dunno, Mister,' the black rider yelled. 'An' I ain't that interested in findin' out that I aim to stop and ask 'em.'

They galloped on again for a few minutes, then Redburn leaned over toward Marshall.

'Where are we headed for?' he called.

He heard the black rider chuckle and marveled at the man's lightheartedness, also his apparent lack of fear.

'You're jest 'bout the doggonedest, askingest man I ever met,' yelled Marshall. Then, 'I'm leavin' you, Mister, soon's we reach them foothills.'

'Leaving me? What for?'

'What for? Yuh damned fool,' Marshall cried, 'Dont'cha wanna live? Them buzzards'll figure you and me's in cahoots. If they catch you, they'll swing you higher'n a kite. That's what for.'

'But what about you?' Redburn demanded.

'Hell, nuthin' will happen to me,' Marshall answered. 'When we get to them hills, you keep ridin', savvy? I'll hold 'em off long enough for you to get outta their reach. Then I'll high-tail.'

'Nothing doing,' Redburn called.

'Doggone it,' Marshall yelled. 'You do like I said or I'll drill you.'

'I'm sticking with you,' Redburn replied stubbornly. 'If we part company now, I'll never see that watch of mine again. I mean to have it.'

Pistol shots fell thicker and faster now, all around them. It was evident to Redburn that their pursuers realized that once the pursued reached the safety of the hills, the chase would have to be abandoned.

'Ride, Mister,' Marshall yelled.

Redburn lashed his horse again. He had difficulty now in keeping Marshall in sight. Fortunately, there were always the hoof beats of the big black to follow. It was minutes later that Marshall pulled up. Redburn followed suit.

'What now?' he asked.

'There's a trail jest beyond here,' the black rider said quickly. 'Foller it and you'll be all right. So long, Mister.'

He wheeled his horse.

'Git goin',' he said briefly.

'I'm going with you,' Redburn answered quietly.

Bullets sprayed the turf just beyond them. Redburn's horse reared up on his hind legs. He fought desperately to check the horse's fright. Marshall swung his horse closer. He stood up in his stirrups, seized the bridle of Redburn's horse.

'Whoa, boy, whoa,' he cried.

The pursuing posse was not far off now.

Turning, desperately, Redburn caught a fleeting glance of an onrushing horde, more formidable in the darkness because their figures loomed larger in the shadows. Marshall dug his spurs into his horse's flanks. The big black bounded forward again, his rider guiding him with one hand, his other holding fast to Redburn's bridle. After a few minutes the latter's mount subsided. They swung into a defile. Marshall slid out of the saddle, his rifle in his hands.

'Git down, Mister,' he yelled.

He whacked the big black with open hand. The horse clattered away and out of sight. Redburn dismounted. His horse galloped away after Marshall's. The latter grabbed Redburn by the arm and fairly dragged him down behind a huge boulder.

'Keep your head down, Mister,' he told Redburn. 'We'll give 'em a taste o' lead and mebbe they'll back up. Then mebbe we'll git a chance to sneak away.'

Redburn crouched down as Marshall had instructed. Bullets whined overhead, sang merrily as they ricocheted from the surrounding rocks.

'Them buzzards are all over the place,' he heard Marshall say. Then. 'They're spreadin' out. Well, this oughta teach 'em somethin'.'

The rifle cracked twice. There was a cry

44

from somewhere beyond them. The black rider chuckled.

'They won't get too reckless now,' he said.

That the posse was now settling down to a real siege was soon evident for bullets splattered from all directions. Suddenly there was a lull, then they heard a loud voice.

'You, Marshall,' cried the voice.

'Yeah?'

'Hold your fire and send out that other feller,' the voice directed.

Marshall tapped Redburn on the shoulder.

'You heard 'im, Mister,' he said briefly. 'This is your last chance to git away with a whole skin.'

'Tell 'em to go t'hell,' Redburn replied.

The black rider laughed.

'Hey,' he yelled to the unseen voice.

'Is he comin'?'

'Nope,' came Marshall's laconic reply. 'This gent is kinda fussy about makin' new friends in the dark.'

A crash of rifles gave Marshall his answer. He fired back, reloaded his rifle and nudged Redburn again.

'I gotta scheme, Mister,' Marshall said briefly. 'Reckon you can take over here while I get busy? I ain't askin' yuh to shoot anybody; jest keep firin' up in the air so's they won't take it into their fat heads to rush us till

45

I get set. Are you willin'?'

'Certainly,' Redburn answered promptly.

'Here's the rifle, Mister. Do jest like I said and we'll have some fun with them galoots.'

He handed Redburn the rifle. Redburn arose, but Marshall pushed him down a bit.

'Don't stick your head up, Mister,' he cautioned him. 'Them buzzards can shoot.'

He slipped past Redburn and crawled away in the dark. Redburn fingered the rifle. He raised it and fired. He counted ten and fired again. He fired four times when he heard a clatter of iron hoofs somewhere behind him. He turned quickly. Marshall stepped up to him.

'We'll see how all-fired smart them galoots are,' the black rider said.

He turned and whipped out one of his Colts and fired twice. There was the unmistakable, high-pitched cry of a frightened horse, then the loud clatter of hoofs of a pitching, scrambling horse. The hoof beats grew louder for a moment, then they both heard the splash of a heavy body striking water.

'Don't breathe,' Marshall whispered, his iron fingers gripping Redburn's arm.

They heard a low cry somewhere beyond them in the darkness, then loud shouts followed by a clatter of horses. Iron rang out against stone and horsemen clattered past

46

them. They heard a loud voice, then the voice that had talked with Marshall.

'After 'em boys,' the voice ordered. 'They're fordin' the river. Let's get 'em this time.'

More horsemen clattered by, not more than a dozen feet away from where the two men crouched, until finally the entire posse had swept past toward the river. They heard heavy bodies strike water, heard varied cries. Then everything faded away. Marshall chuckled. He got to his feet, relieved Redburn of the rifle and scrambled out from behind the shelter of the boulder.

'When them galoots catch up with your cayuse, Mister,' Redburn heard him say, 'we'll be far away.'

Redburn stepped out.

'Come on, Mister,' the black rider called. 'Mind your step now.'

Marshall's hand shot out. Redburn caught it, steadied himself and scrambled to even ground. He was glad that it was getting lighter now. He dashed after Marshall. Minutes later they heard the friendly neigh of the big black. Marshall shoved the rifle into its sheath on the saddle.

'We'll ride double,' he said shortly. 'Git aboard, Mister.'

Redburn mounted with alacrity. Marshall

took the reins, swung up too, in front of him. Presently the big black moved off. He was indeed a powerful animal, more powerful than Redburn had believed. He cantered out toward the open plains again, then again under Marshall's guiding hands, lengthened his stride and broke into a brisk run.

It was probably an hour later that the veil of darkness lifted completely from the prairie. They had covered much ground Redburn estimated, for now, as he turned in the saddle and looked back, the distant hills in which they had taken refuge were but faintly outlined against the brightening morning sun. The big black slackened his pace and simply jogged along. Presently they halted. Marshall dismounted. Redburn alighted too.

Marshall turned and trudged to higher ground, Redburn following at his heels. Marshall halted and pointed. Redburn crowded past him. Below them lay a valley, the brightest, sunniest, flower-sprayed valley that Redburn had ever seen. There was a towering rim of encircling canyon walls around the valley, shutting it out from the rest of the tumultuous world. Redburn's eyes swept the place. He spied a tiny cabin nestling beneath a tall, wide-spread tree. It was almost fantastic, a world set apart, with bright green grass and no barren spots such as abounded in the rolling prairie lands.

'It's Paradise,' he said briefly.

Marshall nodded. He turned away, strode back to his horse, then followed Redburn into the saddle. They skirted the valley and followed a steep, winding trail; a trail so steep that Redburn turned to Marshall questioningly, almost unbelievingly, when the horse started downward. The big black kept his feet with surprisingly little difficulty. Then suddenly, almost before Redburn realized it, they were on level ground again. He turned quickly in the saddle and looked back. He shook his head doubtfully. It seemed unbelievable that they had negotiated that steep trail. He looked twice before he was willing to accept it as a fact. They halted again shortly. Marshall turned to Redburn.

'This is my stampin' ground, Mister,' he said quietly. 'You'll be meetin' my sister soon. What she don't know 'bout me won't hurt her none, savvy?'

Redburn nodded understandingly.

'There's jest one more thing,' the black rider added. 'Like I said before, I'm Ned Harris. How I come to be called Marshall, well, that ain't important right now. I'm trustin' yuh, Mister, to be careful o' your tongue. That's all.'

The big black went on again, this time at a

49

gallop. Marshall put his fingers to his lips and whistled shrilly. There was no answer, nor was there any sign to indicate that his signal had been heard. He whistled a second time, louder, a whistle that echoed through the sunlit valley. Suddenly the cabin door was thrown open and the slim figure of a girl stepped out. For a moment she shaded her eyes from the bright sun with one graceful hand. She spied the big black and waved happily. Marshall waved back.

They clattered up to the door and dismounted. The girl came forward to meet them, to receive Marshall's kiss upon her cheek. Redburn halted and busied himself trying to brush some dust from his clothes.

'Mister,' he heard Marshall call.

He swept off his hat and stepped forward. Suddenly he halted and stared hard. The girl stared hard too, then she gave a glad cry.

'Harry!'

'Oh, Ann!' he cried.

Then she was in his arms, clinging to him and sobbing on his breast.

CHAPTER FIVE

Smith swayed drunkenly against the boulder. There was a deepening haze forming in his eyes. His head throbbed and a thin stream of blood surged down his forehead and cheek and stained his shirt. He tried to raise his right arm but desisted when a sharp pain wracked his body and shoulder.

'Busted,' he mumbled to himself.

He looked down and stared at the Colt still clutched in the rapidly numbing fingers of his right hand. As he watched, the Colt slid out of his hand to the ground. He closed his eyes and rested and hoped that when he opened them again the haze would be gone. Presently he opened his eyes again. The haze was still there. Then he realized that the haze was blood from his wounded head. He raised his left hand, grinned when he found that it was all right, and shoved a second Colt into its holster. He drew his sleeve across his eyes and wiped the blood away.

He stared for a moment at a limp, strangely sprawled figure on the ground in front of him. There was another huddled figure some feet beyond that one. Smith grinned fleetingly. He'd gotten that fellow with his first shot. The second man, the one who lay just in front of the boulder, had proved to be a tough customer. Smith and he had fired point-blank at each other. There was a third figure sprawled out on the ground far beyond the other two. That puzzled him. He frowned and tried to figure out how the third man had gotten there. Then he remembered. Yes, there'd been three men. Two of them had come within range of his guns. The third fellow? He couldn't understand it. Neither could he think about him again. His head throbbed and swam.

Then he remembered the girl. He shifted his body against the boulder, winced with pain and tried to turn so that he could see beyond the boulder. It was a tremendous and superhuman effort and it made him sag against the boulder and gasp for breath. Funny how a couple of leaden slugs could do things to a man. He told himself that the girl was all right. He'd told her to stay behind the boulder. He was sure that she had obeyed. He tried to call her, summoned his fast-ebbing strength but nothing save a hoarse rumble arose in his blood-flecked throat.

He heard hoofs, heard voices, too, and drew the Colt from his left holster. He shifted his sagging body so that he could shoot freely. He grinned evilly. If there were more they'd soon find out that he was still far from dead. They'd find too that he could pump lead with his left hand just as well as with his right. He raised the gun slowly and fixed his eyes upon the thicket. They'd have to come through there to get him. When they burst through, he'd get them just as he had gotten the others. He was terribly tired now, wished he could sit down for a minute before they came at him. It was an effort too to hold the gun, even with his left hand.

He saw four figures burst through the thicket. His eyes began to play tricks on him now. He laughed for the face on the first man was that of old Joe Cox. It was funny for old Joe was miles and miles away, safe with his precious wagon train. The faces of other men were strangely familiar too. He shook his head to clear his fading eyes and winced with pain. He swayed again, this time away from the boulder. His legs grew weak, buckled under him. It was a new and strange feeling, this standing without the support of legs. The Colt slid out of his hand. There was a cry but he heard nothing for now everything was turning black. He lurched and pitched forward on his face.

Just beyond the huge boulder Carol Hall stirred. There was something damp upon her head; now it shifted to her face. The

53

dampness was cooling and comforting. She breathed deeply, sighed and settled back again. It was probably raining, she told herself; the light, feathery rain of a summer's day. She remembered now. She'd been reading, outstretched upon the soft grass behind the cabin beneath the old cotton-wood tree. She was tired and the gentle rain was refreshing. She'd lie there for a few minutes longer, she decided, then she'd simply have to get up. Presently she stirred again. Her eyes were heavy and she found that it was too much of an effort to open them.

'Easy now, honey,' she heard a voice say.

It was, she told herself, her father. He'd returned from his mine near the gully below the cabin. He worked too hard and she was glad that he had quit so early. She ought to be getting up now, getting his supper for him. Slowly and reluctantly she opened her eyes. It wasn't, she swiftly realized, her father's voice that she had heard. Nor was it her father who was bending over her. The strange, grizzled face of a man looked down into hers. She'd never seen him before.

In his hand was a damp cloth and he mopped her brow with it gently. Then it hadn't been rain that she had felt. There was a strong smell of tobacco about him and she drew away only to stop when she realized that her head was pillowed in the hollow of his arm. She struggled to sit up and he lifted her easily, helped her into a sitting position. Then with great suddenness everything came back to her. She turned frantically toward the boulder where she had seen Smith last. There was no sign of him now. She turned again, quickly, to the old man. He patted her hand reassuringly.

'Smith?' he asked.

She nodded.

'Heck, he's all right.'

'Then he . . . he isn't dead?'

The grizzled man laughed lightly.

'Shucks, no, honey,' he answered. 'One bullet jest creased that hard haid o' his. 'Nother busted his arm. Couple o' weeks an' he'll be jest as good's new.'

He turned his head and nodded toward an outstretched figure in the grass a few feet away. Carol followed his eyes. She could see the upturned boots of a man lying there. It was, she told herself, the man she'd shot. A shudder ran through her. She tried to turn her head away but somehow her eyes strayed back.

'Thet feller's jest 'bout as daid as he'll ever be,' she heard the old man say. 'Reckon he musta run plumb into the barrel o' your rifle. There ain't much left o' his face, but from what I kin make of it, his face weren't much to begin with.' He laughed lightly. 'Ornery critter ef you should ask me, Missy.'

'The others? Those other men?'

He nodded briefly.

'Same's this feller, honey. Daid. All of 'em,' he replied. 'That Smith feller is shore poison with a six-gun, I reckon.'

She heard a step behind her and looked up. A burly man with the rolling gait of a man who had spent much of his life in the saddle strode over. The old man looked up too.

'Reckon we're ready whenever you are, Joe,' the man said.

He looked down at Carol and smiled.

'Good t'see you sittin' up, Ma'm,' he said pleasantly.

'Thank you,' she answered. Then, 'Is he ... is he all right?'

'Smith, Ma'm?'

'Yes.'

'Kinda shaky, I'd say, Ma'm,' he said shortly. 'We've patched 'im up some and I don't suppose you'd call 'im purty, but he'll do.'

'I'd like to get up, please.'

'Sure, Ma'm.'

He held out his hands to her, but the old man whom he called Joe pushed him away.

'Git along, you Pete Grady,' he said gruffly.

56

'Reckon I ain't so old yet that I can't help a mite of a girl git up.' The burly man laughed. The old man lifted Carol to her feet. 'Thar,' he said briefly. 'Jest stand still fer a minute, Missy, till yuh get your bearin's.'

She heard voices close by and turned quickly. Two men appeared, supporting on either side a tall youth with a bandaged head and arm. It was Smith and he grinned sheepishly. His face was drawn and white under the bronze and she wanted to run to him, comfort him.

'Reckon I've made a mess o' things, Ma'm,' he said shortly. 'Didn't aim to get you hurt none, though.'

'I'm not hurt,' she answered indignantly. 'And you didn't make a mess of anything. You're the bravest man I ever knew.'

Old Joe Cox's eyes twinkled.

'His haid's pretty swelled up now, Missy,' he said gravely. 'No tellin' how big it'll git afore we git 'im someplace for restin' and doctorin'.'

Smith managed a weak grin. Burly Pete Grady turned away and strode off through the brush. He returned shortly.

'Found them other fellers' cayuses,' he reported to Cox. 'Reckon we might's well get along, too.'

They heard a clatter of hoofs and Smith's

roan trotted up. Grady took the bridle and led the horse down the incline. It was minutes later when he returned. He passed Carol and Cox on the trail and joined the other two men, Luke and Sam Brown, and helped them carry the wounded youth down to the flat land below.

Carol was helped into the saddle of one of the horses which Grady had 'found.' Smith was lifted aboard the roan. The other men mounted, then with Cox and Carol riding ahead, the party moved off. They rode slowly for the jouncing made Smith wince. At frequent intervals they halted to help Smith ease his aching body.

'Good thing,' Cox told Carol as they jogged along, 'That I decided to hunt up the boy and see what thet's screamin' was about.'

She nodded in agreement.

'Course,' he went on shortly, 'I should hev come back fer 'im sooner. Might have saved yuh both a lot o' trouble with them buzzards. Still, I couldn't hev done it, though.' He paused and grinned. 'Reckon I'm jest as stubborn as he is and both o' us ain't much different from a Missouri mule.'

It was probably half an hour later that Luke Brown cantered up.

'Joe,' he said briefly. 'Cain't we find some place real quick? Smith's kinda tuckered out.

58

He looks bad, too.'

Cox made no answer. He wheeled his horse and rode back to Smith's side. He pulled up sharply and leaned over.

''Smatter, boy?' he asked. 'Pain gittin' worse?'

Smith was bent forward over his horse's neck. He made no answer but groaned through his gritted teeth. Carol edged her mount forward. She rode up close to the roan, looked quickly at Smith and turned to Cox.

'We're torturing him,' she said quickly. 'Isn't there a house or a ranch nearby that we could take him to?'

Cox was silent for a minute, then he shook his head slowly.

'Don't know o' none 'round these parts, Missy,' he said shortly. 'Don't hev ranches out on t'prairie, y'know.' He was silent again for a moment before he continued. ''Twas my idee t' git 'im into town, but that's still a good thurty mile ride.' He looked up at the other men. 'You fellers got any idees?'

Grady looked up.

''Course,' he began, 'if we had one o' your wagons ...' His voice trailed away.

'Well, we ain't,' the old man snapped.

Sam Brown edged his mount into the circle. Sam was the younger of the brothers, sandy-haired, stocky, broad-shouldered and slow of

59

speech. There was something likeable about him, particularly when he smiled.

'Joe,' he drawled. 'Reckon you rec'lect thet place I told yuh 'bout?'

Cox eyed him sharply.

'Whut place?'

Sam grinned fleetingly.

'Thet place I found thet day in the storm,' he said.

Cox thought for a moment, then he nodded vigorously.

''Course,' he answered briefly, 'Reckon you kin find it again?'

Sam nodded.

'I reckon so,' he answered.

'Then git goin',' Cox cried. 'You fellers take the little lady and ride ahead. I'll sorta tag along with this feller.'

Sam, Luke and Grady wheeled their horses away. The latter nodded to Carol who rode up beside him.

'You, Grady,' the old man called.

Grady halted and looked back.

'Reckon you'd better stay here too,' Cox called. 'Might need yuh.'

Grady scowled. He swung away from Carol and jogged back to Smith's side. Sam and Luke wheeled their horses apart and beckoned to Carol who spurred her horse and clattered up to them. Presently they rode off.

Carol turned in her saddle and looked back. Cox and Grady were coming on now, the old man on one side of Smith, Grady on the other. Soon they faded out of sight.

That Sam had 'reckoned' correctly was soon obvious. He guided them away and minutes later pulled up sharply. Carol and Luke halted too. Sam dismounted. Luke helped Carol to the ground, then they followed Sam toward what looked to be the edge of a cliff. They joined him amd looked down. Carol gasped.

'Why it's beautiful,' she said. 'It's like a story-book valley.'

Sam grinned broadly.

'Reckon it is, Ma'm.'

'Who owns it?' she asked.

He shook his head slowly.

'Dunno, Ma'm,' he answered.

'There's a house,' she cried excitedly, pointing. 'Look, there's a horse, too, right at the door. See it?'

The brothers followed her pointing hand and nodded as one.

'How does one get down there?' she asked.

'Thar's a hidden trail back thar a piece,' Sam explained. 'I found it the last time.'

'Come on, then,' Carol said quickly.

Sam led the way. Carol and Luke followed again, at his heels. When they reached the trail, Sam halted and waited for them. They

61

gathered around him and looked down. It was the steepest incline that Carol had ever seen. She turned quickly to Sam.

'But we can't go down that way,' she cried. 'We'd . . . we'd break our necks.'

Sam grinned. He strode back to his horse, removed his lasso from the saddle and trudged back to them. He tied one end of the rope to the stump of a tree close by and sent the rest of the rope slithering down the trail. He stepped past Carol, gripped the rope and started down. Carol and Luke watched him. Minutes later, when he had reached the floor of the valley, they heard him call.

'Come on,' he yelled.

'Reckon that means us,' she heard Luke say.

He stepped to the edge of the cliff and looked down. There was no hesitancy on his part. Sam had done it. Now it was his turn. It was as simple as all that. This, she realized, was the West. Some hardy soul simply blazed the trail and the others that followed at his heels asked no questions nor stopped to consider but went right ahead. He gripped the rope and turned for a moment to Carol, for a last word.

'You foller right behind me, Ma'm,' he said simply. 'I'll be waitin' fer you down thar a piece.'

There seemed to be no question about her coming along too; no doubt of her ability to negotiate the steep descent alone. She too was being taken for granted. He stepped off the cliff and slipped away. She heard stones and gravel clatter down the trail and looked over the edge questioningly. Some twenty feet below she spied Luke. He looked up at her and grinned.

'Come on, Ma'm,' he called.

For a moment she made no answer, simply stared at him, then at the valley below him. She hesitated, wanted to cry out to him to go, that she would wait up there for them to return. Smith's agonized face flashed through her mind. She gritted her teeth, reached for the rope and started down. For a moment, fortunately only a brief moment at that, the rope burned her hand.

It slid through her fingers and she stumbled and lurched, then the rope swung closer and she reached for it frantically and caught it and clung to it desperately. It stopped her short. She looked down at Luke and managed a feeble smile. He nodded, reassuringly. Hand over hand she went down then, turning her back to the valley below, trying to shut out the vision of that sharp incline. Presently she bumped into Luke.

'Thet's it, Ma'm,' she heard him say. 'Jest

crowd again me ef your feet git skitterish. I'll stop yer from goin' too fast. There really ain't much to it.'

She lost her fears then. She managed the rest of the distance without further difficulty although some fifteen feet from the bottom she slid again and 'crowded' into Luke. As he had promised, he stopped her too rapid descent. Then they touched bottom. Sam was waiting for them there. It felt good, comforting, to trod the earth again.

Some distance away they spied the house again and turned toward it. Sam swung over on one side of Carol while Luke took the other, then they trudged off. Once or twice they halted and looked about with interest. The grass was bright, green and alive, and a light breeze rustled through the foliage and brush. There were, however, no barren spots. There were trees all about the place, tall, far-flung trees with sturdy trunks. The house itself nestled beneath a towering oak.

'Reckon I'd better go on alone from hyar,' Sam said suddenly. 'Feller that owns the place might git excited seein' too many people all et one time.'

Carol and Luke halted. They watched Sam go striding on towards the house. Suddenly they saw him halt, saw his hands go up slowly, over his head. Luke mumbled something under his breath. Carol saw a tall, black-clad man, gun in hand, step out from behind a tree. Luke caught Carol by the arm and dragged her out of sight, behind a tree that loomed up close by. She saw that he had drawn his Colt, too.

'Wait,' she cried. 'Don't shoot!'

She brushed past Luke, stepped out again and raced forward. She halted when she reached Sam's side.

'What is it?' she asked, looking from Sam to the tall man in front of him.

'Git,' she heard the black clad man say evenly.

'Please,' she said quickly. 'We have a badly wounded boy up there,' nodding toward the cliff. 'We've got to get him to safety. We really weren't trying to intrude upon your privacy. Won't you try to understand?'

The muzzle of the Colt swung in an arc to include her. Carol heard a light step somewhere behind the man, saw a very pretty young girl come down the path to the house, then the girl halted beside the tall man.

'What is it, Ned?' she asked. 'Who are these people?'

'Dunno, Ann,' he answered briefly. 'But we ain't lookin' for company.'

Carol stepped forward. The girl eyed her questioningly.

'Yes?'

Carol smiled fleetingly.

'I'm Carol Hall. You may have known my father, Fred Hall,' she said simply. 'I've been trying to tell you . . . this gentleman,' nodding toward the black clad man with upraised Colt, 'that we have a badly wounded boy up on the cliff.'

'I see.'

'He simply can't go any further,' Carol continued. 'We've got to get him to shelter. We'd be glad to pay whatever . . .'

The girl stepped forward, past the tall man.

'We don't accept pay for hospitality,' she said quietly, then a warm smile flashed over her face. 'I'm afraid my brother hasn't been very hospitable. Please forgive him.'

Carol smiled.

'Of course.'

'You may bring the wounded boy here,' the girl concluded. 'I'm sure we can find room for him.'

'Thank you,' Carol answered.

She turned to Sam, but he had heard the girl grant permission to bring Smith there and now he was striding away. Along the path Luke fell in beside him and trudged along with him toward the foot of the trail. Carol heard a shout from the cliff, looked up quickly, spied Cox and waved.

66

'If you'll excuse me,' the girl said, 'I'll see to it that a room is made ready.'

She turned and went back toward the house. Midway, another man appeared. The girl and he halted, conversed for a moment, then she went on while he sauntered forward. He halted beside the tall man. The newcomer was pleasant-faced and good-looking. He was no plainsman, Carol noted at a glance. He nodded to her and smiled. The black-clad man holstered his Colt.

It was some twenty minutes later that Smith came down the sharp incline, riding the trail on burly Pete Grady's broad back. Old Joe Cox followed. The Brown brothers joined them, then all four men proceeded to carry Smith forward. The girl appeared again, motioned to Cox to come on. The pleasant-faced man sauntered forward.

'Can I be of assistance?' he asked.

Cox looked at him for a moment, then he shook his head slowly.

'Reckon we kin make it the rest o' the way, Mister,' he answered shortly.

The man nodded and stepped back. As they came abreast of him, the black clad man glanced at Smith, looked at him a second time, this time intently, then he frowned. He turned without a word and strode away toward the black horse idling near the door.

Carol caught the other man's eye and looked at him questioningly. He shrugged his shoulder but made no comment. Together they turned and watched the tall man, saw him reach the horse and vault into the saddle, saw him ride off. When he had disappeared from sight, they followed the four men and their burden to the house. The girl held the door wide until Smith had been carried inside and turned to go, too. Then she halted and came back for a moment.

'It's Miss Hall,' the girl asked, 'isn't it?'

'Yes,' Carol replied. 'Carol Hall.'

The girl smiled.

'Thank you.' She glanced at the man beside Carol. 'Harry, please see that Miss Hall is made comfortable.'

The man nodded pleasantly.

'Of course,' he said simply, then with a smile to Carol, 'The Redburns have always delighted in serving beautiful young ladies. Please command me, Miss Hall.'

He bowed gravely. The girl laughed and disappeared inside the house. Redburn held the door for Carol. She looked at him for a moment, hesitantly.

'May I ask you a question?'

'Why not many?' he asked lightly.

'One will do, thank you. That tall man in black,' she said slowly, paused and shook her

68

head.

'Yes?'

She was silent for a moment.

'Never mind, thank you.'

She stepped across the threshold, halted, somewhat surprised, when he laid his hand upon her arm. She looked at him questioningly.

'What were you about to ask me, Miss Hall?' he asked quietly.

'I've changed my mind about it,' she said coolly.

'I see. That, of course, is a lady's privilege,' he answered gravely. 'May I ask something of you now?'

'Why, yes,' she said, surprise in her voice. 'Certainly you may.'

'Thank you. What you were about to ask me concerns someone very dear to me,' he said. 'As long as you accept the hospitality of this household, will you promise to refrain from asking or speaking of the matter you refuse to discuss now?'

'How did you know what was in my mind?' she asked, a faint smile hovering over her lips.

His eyes were steady and very grave.

'Suppose we call it the process of deduction,' he said quietly.

'You'll have to do better than that,' she countered.

'Very well. I happened to enter a bank in Red Dog some months ago while it was being held up. There was but one other patron present at the time. It was a lady,' he concluded.

'You haven't finished,' she said quietly.

'If you insist. You, Miss Hall, were that lady,' he said quietly. 'Is that better?'

'Yes, much better.'

'Have I your promise?'

'I should be ungrateful indeed were I to refuse it,' she answered, smiling sweetly at him.

He stepped aside, permitted her to enter, then she heard the door close. He took her arm and led her along a short hall. He halted in front of a closed door, opened the door and held it wide.

'The basis of a lasting friendship is understanding,' he said with a smile. 'I think we shall be good friends.'

She smiled at him for a moment.

'I shall look forward to it,' she answered, then the door closed quietly behind her.

CHAPTER SIX

The bright moon hung low in the blue sky; a silvery ball of a moon with the shadowy outline of a human, wrinkled and good-natured face spread across its broad expanse. It seemed to hang just behind the cliffs as if it were peering down into the silent valley below. There was a scattering of stars overhead; tiny, nodding little stars that blinked and shone brightly against the backdrop of blue.

Opposite the cliff, far off in the distance, the blunt, slate canyon walls to the north of the valley loomed higher than ever in the moonlight. The ragged edges of the cliff cast strange, black, odd-shaped shadows into the valley. The canyon walls threw off solid blocks of shadows that blackened their steep sides and the land below them.

Somewhere off in that vast darkness a lonely coyote wailed. In the valley a light breeze rustled through the tall grass and brush. The breeze hummed as it sifted through the swaying branches of the tall trees. Something sleek and furry scampered across the path that led to the house and fled into the shadows beyond. A twig crackled beneath its flying feet, then everything was still again.

Carol Hall sat on the front doorstep. Occasionally she turned toward the slightly opened door behind her and listened. Smith was asleep, had been for more than an hour now. Old Joe Cox had 'fixed him up' and the wounded youth, his strength spent, had been dozing intermittently all day and evening.

At supper Carol had sat on one side of Harry Redburn, Ann on the other. The conversation that made the circuit of the table was guided by Redburn. He was witty and always ready with an anecdote that seemed to fit the situation whenever the talk lagged. The laugh that always followed one of his sallies usually revived the conversation and kept it going again.

After supper, Cox and his men drifted out to the barn behind the house. There were no sleeping quarters for them in the house and Cox had snapped up Ann's hesitant suggestion that they use the barn.

Carol too had left the table. She looked in on Smith and found him asleep. Gently she drew up the blankets high around his neck, then she tiptoed out of the room. There was no sign of Ann or Redburn when she returned to the dining room. There was no one there save an old Indian woman who glanced up at Carol, managed a toothless smile and went on clearing away the supper dishes. The parlor door was slightly ajar and passing, Carol heard voices, first Ann's, then Redburn's bantering tone. She hesitated for a moment, then decided against intruding and continued on outside for a breath of air.

She seated herself on the doorstep. Soon she found herself wondering about Ann and Redburn; wondered how they'd met, wondered too what she was really like. Her thoughts turned back to the day of the bank holdup at Red Dog. The details were a bit confused now, however she clearly recalled that the sheriff had spoken of the bandit as one named Marshall. Strangely enough, since that day she had actually forgotten the incident and the bandit's name, too, then, in a twinkling, thanks to Redburn's prompting in the doorway, both had returned to her. It was quite natural then that she had assumed that Marshall was the name of the black-clad man, Ann's name, too. It was natural that at supper she had turned to Ann to compliment her on the meal they had just finished and started to address her as Miss Marshall. Some strange force gripped her and stilled her tongue before she gave full utterance to the name and she was grateful that she had been saved from what would have been a most embarrassing and awkward moment.

73

She glanced at Redburn and flushed, noted without surprise an expression of reproach on his face. Fortunately Ann had turned at that moment to chat with Cox who sat beside her. Carol was certain that Ann hadn't heard her; certain too that she hadn't noticed the exchange of glances that passed between Carol and Redburn.

She tried now to dismiss the bank affair from her mind, the black-clad man, too, but somehow the latter persisted in returning, bursting into her thoughts with alarming and annoying regularity. She recalled having overheard Ann ask Redburn if her brother had said anything about supper. She had tried to catch Redburn's answer without appearing to be too interested, but he had replied in such a low tone that it escaped her.

Finally, Carol got to her feet and strolled down the path. She was some distance from the house when she heard a step in the darkness. She whirled and looked hard. From the shadows came a tall, sombre figure. Swiftly she drew back, crouched down behind the stump of a nearby tree. As the figure drew nearer she saw that it was the black-clad man. For a moment he halted and looked about, then apparently satisfied that he had been unobserved, strode forward toward the house.

Carol's eyes turned toward the house too.

She noted with surprise that the parlor light had been turned out. The tall man whistled softly, then a second time, but this time a bit louder. Presently, Ann appeared in the doorway. She stood there a moment, motionless, then she spied her brother and marched swiftly down the path. The black-clad man met her halfway, took her by the arm and led her away into the shadows. They halted but a few feet from Carol's place of concealment.

'Ned,' she heard Ann say.

'Sh,' cautioned her brother.

'What is it? Is something wrong?' she asked quickly, anxiety in her voice. 'Where have you been? Why all this secrecy?'

Carol heard his low laugh.

'Doggone it, Ann,' he said shortly. 'You kin ask more questions than one o' them lawyer-fellers.'

'But I must ask questions, Ned,' she answered protestingly. 'You never tell me anything. I'm getting tired of guessing.'

'Look, Ann,' he began. 'There ain't no call for you to git excited, see? I got business to attend to and I figured I'd stop by an' see you 'fore I hit the trail. That's all.'

'But, Ned,' she countered quickly, 'is this business so urgent that you must attend to it right away? It seems to me you're away from

75

home more often than you're home.'

'Ann,' he began again. 'Ain't it enough for me t' tell you that I gotta go 'way without you firin' a hull volley o' questions at me? Did I ever butt into anythin' you wanted t' do?'

Ann was silent for a moment.

'No, Ned,' she replied slowly, 'you never did. You weren't interested enough.'

'Now if that ain't jest like a woman,' he said. 'You kin bet I was interested, aplenty, too, only I figured if you wanted me t' know what you was doin' you woulda told me. When you didn't, I jest figured it weren't none o' my business, and let it go at that.'

'I'd like to believe that, Ned, but I can't. I've spent a whole year here, right in this valley. It's been great fun living like a hermit. Oh, I've had company. I admit it. The trees, the flowers, such as they are, the birds; yes, they've been my companions. But did you notice how lonely I was despite them? Did it ever occur to you that I was miserably unhappy here?' she demanded bitterly.

'Ann...'

'Did it strike you odd that after living in the East and learning to love the comforts that civilization offers, that I should be contented to live here, without any of those comforts? Did it occur to you that something had happened in my life to make me lose interest

76

in it, and that life only began to interest me again after fate directed Harry Redburn here?' she went on.

'Lemme know when you git done, Ann,' he said drily. 'I kin wait.'

'Did it occur to you to ask about Harry, about us? No, Ned, it didn't. But I'll tell you even though it may bore you. Harry and I were engaged. We had a silly quarrel. I came West again, never expecting to see him again. Fate, however, took a hand in things and, well, directed him to you and you brought him here without knowing who he was. There's just one more thing, Ned, and I'll have had my say,' she said.

'I'm listenin',' he said briefly.

'I'm glad that I'm not indebted to you for my schooling, for being able to look back to my life in the East, oh, for everything that was so wonderful,' she said quietly. 'Thank Heaven that Dad left me enough money so that I'll never have to turn to you for anything. You can go now, Ned. Come and go as you please. I'll never question you again.'

She turned away slowly, broken, her head bowed, but Ned caught her arm and halted her.

'Jest a minute, Ann,' he said. 'You've had your say; now I'll have mine. I've been dreadin' this moment, but now that it's here,

I'm kinda relieved. There's somethin' I gotta tell you. 'Twon't be easy, still it'll be heaps easier for both o' us if I tell it 'stead o' havin' somebody else do the tellin'.'

She turned again and faced him, a slim girl whose teary eyes shone brilliantly in the shadows about her.

'Dad lost the ranch, Ann,' he said slowly, 'jest 'fore he died. You don't remember that bank feller in town. Anyway, he tricked Dad into signin' somethin' and then kicked us off the place. Dad didn't leave anything behind. He didn't have anythin' to leave.'

'Ned!' she cried.

'I told you this would hurt,' he said gently. 'Still, you're a grown woman, Ann, an' you gotta right to know now. Anyway, I sent you the money for your schoolin', an' the money for all them other things you've been talkin' 'bout.'

'You?' she asked, incredulity in her voice.

'Yep, Ann,' he answered slowly. 'Me. You'll prob'bly hate me when I git finished tellin' you, but well, it won't matter so much, 'cause when I leave here I ain't never comin' back.'

'Go on,' she commanded in a strangely hollow tone.

'I swore I'd make that bank feller pay everything back. Well, he died 'fore I could

78

do anything. I reckon I musta been pretty crazy when I heard 'bout it, for I didn't care which bank squared things up after that. Every bank was the same t'me. I made 'em all pay for what that feller done,' he concluded.

'But, how, Ned?'

'How?' he laughed coldly. 'The only way I knew.' He tapped the Colts that swung against his thighs.

'You mean . . .' she whispered.

'That I stole their money?' he said harshly. 'Yep, that's jest what I do mean. It was their lives and their money against my Colts and I won. They killed everythin' good and clean and decent in me, took everythin' Dad and I had worked and starved for, took it and then laughed at us. Well, they payed aplenty for what they done.'

'Oh, Ned,' she sobbed and threw herself into his arms.

He held her close and patted her head gently.

'Don't cry, Ann, honey,' Carol heard him say. ''Twasn't your fault what I done. Mebbe it wasn't all mine, either. Anyway, nobody but this Redburn knows and he don't look like the kind that talks without thinkin'. Nobody else knows. Besides, I've been callin' myself Marshall.'

'Marshall?'

'Yep. Y'see, Ann, I played a couple o' them rodeos, ridin' wild broncos. I substituted fer a feller named Marshall. The rodeo folks had been advertisin' Marshall but he never showed up. So they hired me and made me keep workin' under this other feller's name. Folks got to like me and liked the way I rode them ponies, so pretty soon they got to callin' me "Mustang." Well, I got so used t'the name that I kept it. I've been "Mustang" Marshall ever since,' he continued.

'But now, Ned?' she asked. 'What shall we do now?'

'Shucks, Ann,' he said lightly. 'That's easy. You kin marry this Redburn feller and go East with 'im. You've been tellin' me how happy you were there once, I reckon you'll be happy there again.'

'And you?' she pressed.

'Me?' he laughed shortly. 'Heck, Ann, don't you worry none 'bout me. I've been hearin' a lot 'bout California. They tell me it's all new country, big and rich, too. Mebbe that's the place for me. Anyway, I'm kinda anxious to see it.'

'But California's so far away,' she said. 'Why, Ned, I may never see you again if you go there.'

'Quien sabe?' he said lightly, then reassuringly. 'Anyway, Ann, you'll have

Redburn and I reckon he must be some pumpkins back East. Bein' his wife, you'll be somebody. You'll be happy there and you'll soon fergit there was ever anybody like me. Mebbe it'll be better that way.'

'No,' she cried. 'I'll never forget you. I won't go East. I'll follow you to California, anywhere you go. If you're in trouble, Ned, it's my trouble, too. You did those terrible things for me. If only you had told me in time, then perhaps things might have been different.'

'Ann,' he said slowly, 'You're makin' things harder for me. You do just like I said. Then mebbe someday, somehow, someplace, we'll meet again. Then I kin look up, proud-like, y'know, an' say right out, "That's my sister. She's a fine lady."' He paused and patted her arm again. 'Reckon I'd better be goin', Ann.'

She clung to him again, her eyes searching his shadowed face.

'No? So soon?' she pleaded. 'Ned, we've just found each other. We were strangers before tonight. You mustn't go now. I won't let you.'

He turned slowly and faced the house.

'For a year, Ann, I've been hidin', jest because o' one feller, a ranger. This morning I saw 'im again,' he said quietly.

'This morning, Ned?' her voice was barely

above a whisper now.

He nodded grimly. Unconsciously, his hands fell away from her and came to rest upon the butts of the Colts.

'He's the slickest, smartest ranger they got. Reckon that's why they sent 'im after me,' he added briefly. 'What makes it funny is that right now he's in my house, sleepin' in my bed, and eatin' my grub while I gotta hide out.'

'Ned, you don't mean that wounded boy, that Smith?' she asked quickly.

He nodded briefly.

'Yep, that's the one, Ann. Only his name ain't Smith. It's Smith Jenkins. His old man was that bank feller I've been tellin' you 'bout,' he concluded quietly. 'I'm goin', Ann.'

They heard a light step somewhere in the shadows beyond them. Ned pushed Ann away and stared hard into the night. His hands gripped his Colts, his tensed body bent forward, alert.

Carol saw a shadowy figure step past her, saw the metallic gleam of a drawn Colt. She clapped her hand over her mouth to stifle the scream that arose in her throat. She stared hard and gasped for the shadowy figure wore a white bandage around his head. It was the youth named Smith.

'Reach,' she heard Smith say.

He had circled around and now his Colt had halted in the hollow of Ned's back. Slowly the black-clad man's hands climbed skyward.

Successful though he had been, the effort proved costly to Smith. He was still weak and he braced himself by spreading his tired legs. His hand was unsteady. He swayed momentarily, braced himself again and laughed strangely. It wasn't the boyish Smith that Carol had come to know. This was another Smith, a stranger, a lawman, a man who hunted other men, a man with a strange voice and a cold, deadly laugh. He swayed again drunkenly, then the Colt slid out of his hand to the grass.

He stared hard at it for a moment, raised his head slowly, numbly, stared at Ann, her brother, then at Carol who had risen and stepped out from behind the stump of the tree. Slowly, before their startled eyes, he crumpled. Carol screamed. She leaped forward only to halt when Ann caught her arms and gripped her tightly.

'You,' Ann said coldly, furiously. 'You eavesdropper!'

She drew back her hand and struck Carol across the mouth. Carol staggered. Mechanically she put her hand to her mouth. Slowly she drew it away and stared hard at it, almost incredibly. Her fingers were wet, stained with blood drawn from her own lips. Numbly she looked at Ann, at the tall black-clad man beside Ann, then slowly she swept past them and trudged away into the shadows.

CHAPTER SEVEN

Old Joe Cox sat up in his bunk, shook his muddled head and listened. He had heard voices, a scream, the sound of running feet. Now he heard nothing.

'Jest when a feller gets to dreamin',' he mumbled half-aloud, 'some folks gotta wake 'im up.'

He bumped his head against a loose board in the tier above him and cursed roundly. He rubbed his head and considered for a moment, then he sighed, and swung his booted feet over the side of the bunk and dropped to the floor. He dropped his hat, groped for it in the darkness, found it and jammed it down upon his head. He straightened up, took another hitch in his sagging gun-belt and trudged toward the door.

A sleepy, heavy voice from somewhere beyond him in the darkness grumbled angrily.

'Who's zat?' the voice asked.

'A ghost, yuh damned fool,' Cox replied.

'Who's zat?' the voice asked again.

'A ghost,' Cox yelled. 'Can'tcha hear?'

'Oh,' the voice said sleepily. 'G'wan back t'sleep, ghost. It's too late at night to do any haunting.'

Cox stumbled across something and launched a vicious kick at it. When the object refused to give him the right of way, Cox howled with pain. He halted and rubbed his bruised foot tenderly, then he stepped over the object, glared at it over his shoulder and groped his way forward toward the door. He grumbled again, this time about nothing in particular but about things in general. Finally he reached the door. It yielded to his shoulder and flew outward and collided with the side of the barn. Cox fell over the threshold and just barely avoided the swinging door which whipped back and banged against the jamb. He got to his feet. It was chilly and he grumbled about that too.

He looked up toward the house and noted that it was dark. He swung away from the house, skirted it, whipped out his Colt when he saw a shadowy figure stumble along a few feet ahead of him.

'Stan' whar yuh are!' he yelled.

He plunged forward, his gun ready. The figure halted, turned and came toward him. Cox halted too. It came closer and Cox saw

85

with surprise that it was Carol Hall.

'Why, honey,' he said shortly. 'Thet you?'

She made no answer.

'Whar yur goin' this time o' night?' he asked.

'I . . . I don't know,' Carol answered dully.

He looked at her sharply, questioningly, scratched his bristly chin reflectively for a moment. He searched her face, stared hard when he saw tears in her eyes.

'Why, child,' he said presently, 'yuh been cryin'!'

He shoved the Colt into the holster, gripped her shoulders with his two hands and swung her about so that the moonlight bathed her face.

'An' your lip, honey,' he said in surprise. 'It's bleedin'.' His hands tightened on her shoulders. 'Who done thet?' he demanded roughly.

She raised her head slowly, opened her mouth to speak when they heard a clatter of horses' hoofs. He released her, stepped past her for a moment and stared into the darkness beyond them. The clatter of iron on stone grew louder. He drew her into the shadows again. They heard a shout from somewhere in the valley.

'What in thunder . . .' she heard him say, then his voice died away.

86

A band of horsemen swept out of the shadows and whirled toward the house. A volley of shots riddled the walls of the house and smashed the windows.

'Raiders!' Cox yelled.

He caught Carol by the arm and fairly dragged her toward the barn. He threw open the door, shoved her inside, whipped out his Colt and fired twice at the horsemen. Two of them wheeled away from the main party and raced toward the barn, firing as they came. A bullet whined overhead and buried itself in the framework above the door. A second slug whistled past Cox's head and splintered the door. Cox cursed softly and fired twice then he tumbled inside, slamming the door behind him.

One of the horsemen toppled out of his saddle. His horse galloped past the barn and disappeared in the darkness. The second horseman sagged in his saddle, fell forward on his horse's neck. The horse slowed down, jogged toward the barn and halted at the door. His rider slipped out of the saddle and fell heavily to the ground. Once he moved, then he lay still. The horse backed away from the door, wheeled and dashed off after the first horse.

Meanwhile, things were happening elsewhere, though not particularly far away.

At the first sound of hoofs, Ned turned to Ann and nodded grimly toward the house.

'Inside,' he commanded briefly, then in a louder tone, 'Run!'

She whirled and fled up the path. The black-clad rider glanced at the crumpled form of Smith Jenkins. For a moment he hesitated, then he bent swiftly, swung Smith up and over his shoulder and strode quickly up the path and into the house. Ann led the way to the bedroom which Smith had vacated. She came forward quickly and helped Ned lay him upon the bed.

'Keep under cover,' Ned said briefly.

He whipped out his Colts and raced out of the room. He halted momentarily and hammered with his gun butts on Redburn's door, then he stepped quickly to the front door and threw it open. He crouched in the doorway and raised his guns. The clatter of hoofs grew louder, then it was close at hand. He saw a party of horsemen whirl out of the shadows and converge upon the house, riddling the front with a crash of lead. Bullets splintered the door, the jamb, the walls and smashed the windows. He bent lower, then the Colts blazed. Horses and men fell almost in front of the door. Here a riderless horse cantered away. There a horseless man hobbled away painfully, only to totter and finally fall.

Somewhere beyond the house shots rang out. For a moment Ned was puzzled, then he recalled the four men who had carried the wounded ranger into the house. A grin swept his face. The shots indicated that they were taking a hand in the fight too. Someone knelt beside him. He turned quickly. It was Redburn with the startled expression of one who had been rudely awakened from a deep sleep. A gun gleamed in his hand.

'What is it?' he demanded.

'Raiders,' Ned answered briefly, then scornfully. 'Prairie dogs. Them fellers are the ones that gener'ly raid wagon trains. They musta figured this plac'd be easy fer 'em.'

The horsemen had withdrawn into the shadows and he knew that they were reforming their ranks for the second attack upon the house.

'Reckon you'd better git back inside,' he said quietly. 'This ain't your fight, Mister.'

Redburn made no answer. Instead, he crouched down beside Ned, raised his gun and waited. Ned glanced at him curiously for a moment, then he turned away. The second onslaught was not long in coming. There was a rush of pounding hoofs, then the attackers swarmed forward again. This time, however, they swung past the house in open order instead of converging upon it. Lead splattered

89

the house, the doorway and the smashed windows again.

Three guns barked in unison from the darkened doorway. Here a rider lurched in his saddle and crashed into the grass. Beyond him a horse screamed and plunged to earth, pinning his rider beneath him. Here a wounded horse plunged toward the house, bringing his frantic rider directly in range of the black-clad man's murderous Colts. A bullet jerked the horseman upright in his saddle. A second slug hurled him to the ground. His horse whined and hobbled away.

In the barn Cox had roused his men, routed them out of their bunks and now they were crowding around him, waiting impatiently for him to order them into the fray. In a distant corner of the barn, Carol Hall crouched. Old Joe had led her there himself and ordered her to stay there. He was crouching at the door now, listening. The Brown brothers and big Pete Grady were there too.

'Kinda quiet now,' Cox mused.

Hardly had his words died away when a roar of shots echoed through the valley. Old Joe's eyes narrowed.

'Must be aplenty in thet gang,' he said shortly, then scornfully, 'damned hellions.'

Luke Brown nudged him.

'Mebbe we could kinda sneak up on 'em,

Joe,' he said, hopefully. 'We might be able t'drive 'em off an' then make a break fer the house.'

'Mebbe,' Cox said briefly.

Burly Pete Grady leaned forward.

'Ain't but one man up thar,' he said, nodding toward the house, 'An' he don't look like much.' Then adding apologetically, 'leastways, not with a six-gun.'

Cox got to his feet. His guns were in his hands.

'Let's go,' he said simply.

He kicked open the door and stepped outside.

'Come on,' he yelled over his shoulder.

The others piled out. Guns in hands they pounded along at Cox's heels. There were tall trees up ahead of them and Cox headed for them.

'Git down behind 'em,' he yelled.

He dropped down behind a tree, glanced at the others and noted that they had done so, too.

'Hol' your fire,' he called.

They heard racing hoof beats somewhere beyond them in the darkness. Presently they grew louder.

'They're comin'!' Grady yelled.

'Don't shoot till they're between us an' the house,' Cox ordered.

Now the horde of horsemen swept down again, bursting out of the shadows and into the open. In the moonlight Cox counted at least sixteen of them.

'Shoot!' he yelled.

A volley of bullets poured out from behind the trees. Horses screamed, reared and plunged forward again. Here a horse plunged into the grass, throwing his rider over his head. The man rolled over and climbed to his knees. A bullet flattened him on the ground. Other riders tumbled out of their saddles, and off to a side, riderless horses pounded away.

'Let's go,' Cox yelled.

The others followed hard at his heels as he led the way toward the house. Their Colts roared as they ran. In front of the house a group of horsemen wheeled their mounts frantically and strove mightily to get out of the line of fire. Colts blazed from the darkened doorway and horses screamed with pain. One horse reared up on his hind legs and crashed over backwards, crushing his rider beneath him. Another horse sank to his knees, sagged and toppled over. His rider managed to free his feet from the stirrups, whirled and clutched at the bridle of a riderless horse that galloped past. Miraculously, the man swung himself into the saddle. He spied the four men dashing toward the house, wheeled and bore down upon them. Cox's guns belched fire. The horse went down. The man pitched forward over the horse's head. He struggled to his knees. Cox's guns blazed. The man spun and plunged headlong into the grass.

Sam and Luke Brown, bringing up the rear, slowed down and fired aimlessly into the whirling mass in front of the house. Luke cursed when a bullet whisked his hat from his head; ducked instinctively and just in time, too, when a second slug whistled past him. He grabbed his brother and fairly dragged the stocky Sam along.

'Come on,' Luke yelled. ''Tain't healthy hyar.'

'Leggo,' Sam yelled, twisting and squirming.

'Git along,' Luke answered doggedly.

'Doggone yuh, Luke,' Sam panted over his shoulder. 'Why'd yuh do thet? Kinda reco'nized a cuss I've been trailin' fer a year an' jest when I'm throwin' down on 'im, yuh gotta horn in.'

'Hell with 'im.'

'Oh, yeah? Thet's the feller what stole yo' pants,' Sam yelled.

Luke came to a sudden halt.

'Doggone yuh, Sam,' Luke yelled. 'Why'n hell didn't yuh say so?'

A bullet whistled and sped between them.

Both put on a spurt and piled into the house. Two men who were crouching in the darkened doorway backed away to permit them to enter. Sam tripped and plunged into someone who went down underneath him. Luke fell on top of Sam. There was general confusion for a minute, then they unscrambled themselves.

Grady, they quickly noted, had taken his place at one of the smashed windows. He crouched and raised his Colt and each time that he fired, he grunted audibly. When he missed, he swore roundly. Sam crowded past him, made his way forward toward another window, dropped to one knee, found a target and fired. Presently he laughed and turned around.

'Hey, Luke,' he called.

'You hit?' Luke asked anxiously from the dark.

Sam laughed lightly.

'Naw,' he answered. 'Jest wanted t'tell yuh thet I got thet feller. Doggone ef he ain't wearin' yo' pants, too.'

Now the firing seemed to die down. Soon they heard the raiders galloping off. Sam and Grady got to their feet and busied themselves reloading their Colts.

'Do you think they'll come back?' a voice asked. They recognized it as Redburn's.

'Mebbe,' came Cox's noncommittal reply.

There was a momentary silence after that, then Grady began to sniff.

'Somebody smell somethin'?' he asked.

'Nope,' Cox answered.

'Doggone it, I do,' Grady insisted.

Cox sniffed loudly.

'Gunpowder,' he said briefly.

'Thet ain't what I'm smellin' right now,' Grady said doggedly.

Sam Brown sniffed the air for a moment.

'Jest a minute, fellers,' he said. 'Damned ef I don't smell somethin', too.' He was silent for a moment, then he yelled, 'Hey, somethin's burnin'!'

'Thet's what I been smellin',' Grady cried, triumphantly. 'They're tryin' to burn us out!'

There was a general rush toward the door. A volley of shots spattered the doorway, Luke coughed and went down on all fours.

'Git back,' Cox cried. 'It's a trick t' git us out into th' open!'

Sam and Grady dragged Luke back into the room. The others crouched down in the darkness.

'Luke,' Sam said anxiously. 'Yuh hit bad?'

There was no answer.

'Luke,' Sam pleaded. 'Yuh hear me?'

'Easy, boy,' Grady said shortly. 'Joe,' he alled. 'Com'ere, willya?'

Old Joe Cox groped his way toward them.

95

Grady moved away.

'Is he . . . is he daid?' they heard Sam ask in a small voice.

'Daid hell,' they heard Luke say. He coughed and spat viciously. 'Some cock-eyed polecat blowed m' teeth down m' throat.'

There was another violent burst of firing now. Lead splattered the front of the house again, plowed through the walls, tore huge splinters from the framework around the paneless windows and shattered the door jamb. No one needed an order from Cox now. As one all hands edged forward to the windows and door. Presently they began to answer the withering fire, aiming at the flashes of the raiders' guns. Here someone grunted as he fired; there someone cursed when he missed. Now the smell of smoke grew more pronounced.

'Joe,' Grady yelled suddenly. 'Thet damned fire's gettin' worse. Betcha them hellions done fired the barn!'

They heard Cox gasp.

'The barn! Thet's it.' Then loudly, 'Thet girl's in thar! Git outta my way!' he roared.

Burly Pete Grady grabbed him and smothered him in a bear-like hug.

'Hol' on, Joe,' he cried. 'Yuh'll never make it alive. Them hellions'll blow yuh apart the minute yuh step out thar!'

There was a sudden movement in the doorway. A tall, shadowy figure that blended with the night leaped out and disappeared.

'Who was thet?' someone asked.

There was no answer, nothing but a strange, nervous, hollow chuckle from the shodowy figure they recognized as Redburn.

'Funny,' the voice mused again. 'Coulda swore that was somebody over thar not more'n a minute ago.'

There was no burst of firing outside now, although everyone waited for it, expectantly, breathlessly, and tensed; waited for it to come, to let them know that the raiders had spotted the black figure. Far off in the night someone screamed, then a strange, drawn-out silence followed. Someone sighed in the darkness of the room, relaxed and laughed lightly, the laugh of one who had bridged disaster.

'Reckon he musta made it,' the voice said simply.

No one answered.

'Sam,' Luke called presently.

'Yeah?'

'That feller with m' pants. Kin yuh see 'im?' Luke asked.

They heard Sam chuckle.

'Shore kin, Luke,' he answered. 'But they

ain't no good now. They're full o' bullet holes!'

CHAPTER EIGHT

Ned Harris leaped out of the doorway and promptly disappeared in the darkness. His black garb blended so perfectly with the night that he became part of it, an intangible shadow that moved swiftly within other shadows. He bent low and kept close to the house, taking full advantage of the black background the house presented. Once or twice he hurdled limp and grotesquely sprawled figures. They were the men who had fallen beneath his fire and that of the plainsmen under Cox. Here and there dead horses lay on their sides, their legs stiffened in death and now strangely rigid in mid-air. He glanced fleetingly at the brush that faced the house.

Behind the brush crouched the raiders. He noted their unmistakable shadows in the dim light that filtered through the brush; shadows which his keen eyes speedily recognized and dissolved into men. They crouched, impatient and lustful, waiting for an opportunity to strike.

When it had become apparent that the

defenders of the house had no intention of sallying forth in an effort to dislodge and drive off the attackers, trickery was resorted to. First, the raiders' horses were ridden away. This was done to create the impression that the raiders had been driven off and that it was safe for the defenders to venture out. Of course the main body of raiders was carefully hidden away behind the brush ready to swarm over the defenders should they step outside. When this stunt failed to bring about the desired effect, a second trick was resorted to.

The barn was set afire. The raiders lay back and waited for the defenders to rush out and attempt to save it from total destruction. However, there was no outpouring of men and the raiders waited and cursed, and the longer they waited, the more they cursed.

Both of these methods of attack and massacre dated back to the Indians who had introduced them in their attacks upon unwary and inexperienced settlers. Both had proven highly successful; so successful that the settlers borrowed them and adapted them to their own uses. When parties of settlers bent upon avenging their dead swooped down upon Indian villages, the same tricks were resorted to and worked to a nicety upon their originators. The Indians, historians claim, were so dismayed that they promptly abandoned these tricks. White raiders resurrected them and incorporated them in their own plans of attack.

It had been decided to rush the house. The weight of the attackers' numerical superiority was expected to overwhelm the defenders. Upon a given signal, the raiders burst through the brush and plunged forward toward the house. Unfortunately for them they abandoned the Indian method of approach, that of stealth and quiet. Instead they blazed away at the house and sent a roar of gunfire echoing through the valley. Ned Harris heard the roll of thundering gunfire. He was too close to the barn to turn back now. Grimly he plunged on, dependent upon Cox and his men to repel the attack.

The roar of shots brought the defenders back to their posts on the run, all save Luke Brown who was ready long before the onslaught began. He had drifted over to one of the shattered windows, squatted down and felt tenderly of his lacerated gums. He cursed the raiders and their ancestors, turned and spat out of the window, gulped and swallowed hard when he saw them swarm out of the brush. He dropped to his knees.

'Hey!' he yelled.

He whipped out his guns and blazed away with both hands. Sam came rushing over to take his place beside Luke. Promptly, Sam's guns went into action too. Pete Grady opened fire from the other window, while old Joe Cox shoved Redburn away from the door and took a hand in the proceedings. Redburn refused to accept Cox's action as final. He dropped down, found room for his arms and gun in a limited sphere close to the bottom of the door and opened fire.

The roar of gunfire was deafening. Smoke filled the room. The raiders were riddled in their tracks, and tossed aside like stalks of wheat in a threshing machine. One raider, considerably fleeter of foot than his fellows, managed to weather the deadly fire from the house and actually reached a point within stepping distance from the door when Cox caught sight of him. He swung around but before he could bring his Colts into action, Redburn's gun roared and blasted the man away. Cox glared at Redburn resentfully, but in the darkness Redburn failed to notice it. The surviving raiders broke and retreated and fled for their lives to the comparative safety of the brush. Once behind the brush they continued the gun fight.

The attack simplified matters for Ned Harris. The raiders were too occupied with the defenders of the house to notice him. He raced past the house, past the trees from behind which Cox and his men had poured a withering fire into the ranks of the onrushing horsemen earlier. He soon reached the burning barn, halted for a moment to take in the situation. Flames, he noted at a glance, were sweeping hungrily from the front of the barn toward the rear. The front of the barn was a sheet of flame. Entry through the door was an impossibility.

He swung away, skirted the barn, reached the rear of the structure and hunted frantically for a loose board. He found one presently, tugged at it with all his strength. Finally it broke, came away. He tossed it away and plunged into the barn.

The smoke was heavy and progress necessarily slow. He halted once or twice to get his breath which became labored. He groped his way to a corner, fought a moment for air, stepped again and tripped over something that groaned beneath him. He fought his way to his feet, swept the limp form of Carol Hall into his arms and retraced his steps. The last few feet were the most difficult. He was choking, gasping for breath and the girl's dead weight made things harder. He gave a mighty surge, felt the blood drain out of his face and head, felt an iron band tighten around his chest and knew instinctively that he would have to reach the open air within the next minute or he was through. His head seemed strangely light and hollow and a curious rumbling, like a mountain cascade rushing down a spillway, filled his ears. He wanted to cry out but a heavy hand gripped his throat. He plunged forward blindly, then suddenly he burst into the open. He stumbled weakly, choked, and fell to his knees. There was no strength, no feeling in his arms and the unconscious girl slid away to the ground. He sagged and fell forward on his hands. Doggedly he huddled there, fighting for his breath, then slowly he began to suck in the cool air like a huge, shaggy buffalo he had seen once drinking from a mountain stream.

It was difficult getting to his feet again, but he forced himself up, swayed drunkenly for a moment, braced himself by spreading his legs, bent and lifted the girl. He halted for a moment, to draw a deep breath then he swung her up, now higher, still higher, then a mighty effort swept her up into his arms, safe in his tightening grasp. The blood surged back into his face and head and caused a strange, tingling sensation in his temples.

Now a plan began to take form in his brain. He started foward slowly, quickened his pace as he felt new strength flowing into his body. He plunged ahead recklessly, fought his way through the thick brush that clawed at his face and clothes. The unconscious girl's bowed head rested against his chest and his hand shielded her face from the sharp briars. Once or twice he stumbled and nearly went down but each time he managed, always beyond understanding, to steady himself and keep his feet. Soon he noticed that the rumbling in his ears had died away completely. Instead he heard the roar of gunfire somewhere behind him, but as he trudged on even that began to fade in the distance.

Earlier he had tethered his horse in a hidden ravine. He slowed down and looked about him, trying to place the spot in the dark. He whistled softly; whistled a second time louder and longer, then from out of the shadows ahead came his answer, a shrill neigh. Minutes later he reached the rim of the ravine, slid down and came to an abrupt halt at the horse's side. He hoisted the girl into the saddle, held her there with one hand while he swung up behind her. She sank back against him. He wheeled the big black, guided him up the bank of the ravine. When they reached level ground again, he gathered the reins in his left hand and drew his gun. He galloped back toward the house.

At a distance of about one hundred yards from the house, he halted, fired twice in the direction of the brush that sheltered the raiders. After a minute's pause he went on, fired twice again, then he heard shouts. He saw shadowy figures burst out of the brush and run toward him. He swung his horse around and cantered away. Bullets whined overhead. He pulled up and waited till he heard horses' hoofs behind him. He reloaded the empty chambers of the Colt. Now the shadows on horseback came closer. He made no attempt to fire, simply galloped on and glanced back from time to time to see that he was still being pursued. When he was satisfied that his plan had succeeded, that he had drawn the raiders away from the house and in pursuit of him, he was content. He held the big black in check for he knew that it would be a simple matter for him to outdistance the raiders. There was no need of that yet. When he reached the hills, miles and miles away, he would show his pursuers what the big black could really do once he was given his head.

Suddenly the figures of two horsemen loomed up on a ridge ahead of him. For a moment he frowned. Could it be that the raiders had outsmarted him, that they had outflanked him, that now he would be caught between two fires? The pursuing raiders were too close for him to hesitate. The Colt blazed suddenly. One of the horsemen disappeared as though a powerful hand had wafted him out of the scene. The big black bounded forward. The Colt belched fire again, a third time. Now there was no one ahead of him. He heard the ringing clatter of hoof beats behind him, spurred the big black and sent him on faster. Presently he checked his horse. It would never do for him to discourage his pursuers so early in the chase. He pulled back on the reins.

Suddenly a hand lifted the veil of darkness from the land. Ahead of him lay the prairie, beyond that, the tall and still shadowy hills. Gradually the shadows faded away and soon the rugged hills stood out boldly against the sky. He turned in his saddle and glanced back. Now he could see six horsemen strung out behind him in single file. He grinned fleetingly. Soon he would be leading them into the hills, in through narrow passes, along steep, winding, treacherous trails where a single mis-step might plunge a horse and rider into space and down upon the rocks hundreds of feet below.

He saw the flashes of the raiders' guns, heard their bullets whistle past harmlessly. Once he was tempted to return their fire but he checked himself and shoved the Colt into his holster. The girl stirred once or twice, moaned, then she lay still again. The big black loped along, holding his pace easily. The pursuers spread out and two of them raced ahead like ends going downfield to cover a long punt. Ned laughed lightly. The uneven ground made flanking an impossibility and he knew that soon the single file formation would have to be resumed. They kept up a steady fire. Sometimes a single man would fire. Other times all six men would fire together.

Now they were entering the hills. The big black horse's hoofs clattered over rock and shale. He swung through a shaded pass, galloped over a narrow, nature-made bridge of rock and followed a winding trail uphill. Harris heard the raiders enter the pass, heard the ring of iron on stone, noted that they slowed to a walk when they reached the bridge. Once he glanced upward at the hills and nodded to himself. Minutes later he pulled up, slipped out of the saddle, lifted the girl and carried her off to a tiny grass plot of ground and laid her down. The big black trotted up too. There were huge boulders beyond and Harris ran to them, searched behind them until he found a package which he tore open. There were two sticks in the package. He shoved one stick into his belt and hurriedly raced away.

He halted at the edge of a tall cliff and looked over. Directly below him was the stone bridge. He glanced once at the line of raiders making their way up the treacherous trail. He drew back his arm and threw the stick. There was a thunderous roar followed by a tremendous crash. Dirt and rock filled the air. He whipped out the second stick and threw it too. Another giant explosion echoed through the hills. Again dirt and rock sailed high in the air. Presently he peered over the edge again. Where once there had been a bridge there was nothing, nothing now but a huge, impassable void. The dynamite had removed the raiders' only means of retreat. That it had done the same for him meant little. He was not going back.

There was still another chore to be done before the work was completed. Huge boulders stood at the head of the trail. Harris scrambled forward. Just below him plodded the raiders. He put his shoulder to one boulder. It moved slightly. He turned and whistled shrilly. The big black raised his head. Harris seized the bridle, wheeled the horse and backed him against the boulder. For a moment the big black rebelled. He snorted, reared up on his hind legs and struck out viciously with his forelegs. Harris backed away. He spoke softly to the horse. The big black subsided. Harris gripped the bridle again and backed him against the boulder. The powerful hind legs of the horse dug deep into the ground. There was a crunching sound, the sound of something being uprooted, torn from its moorings. The boulder moved, rolled forward a few feet and came to a halt. Harris glanced at it quickly and nodded briefly. The trail was completely blocked off now. There could be no escape from either end. he laughed coldly, patted the big black's sleek neck. From the trail below he heard shouts, then shots. He laughed again, vaulted into the saddle and jogged off.

Carol Hall was sitting up, her head in her hands, when he halted beside her. She turned slowly, glanced first at the horse, then her eyes came up. For a moment she stared hard at him. He knew in an instant that she had recognized him.

'Did you ... did you bring me here?' she asked.

He nodded gravely.

'What are you going to do with me?' she asked.

His eyes swept her face. She was pretty; prettier than any girl he'd ever seen before. A girl had to be pretty to look that good after the terrifying experience she had had.

'Well?' she asked shortly.

'Dunno yet,' he answered.

She wished he wouldn't just sit there and look at her. He had a curious way of looking through one. His eyes never faltered, not for a moment. It was disconcerting and made the one he looked at, turn away. She turned and looked up at the hills. They seemed bleak and cold and uninviting. Beyond the hills she could see tall peaks, snow-capped peaks that towered high into the pale blue sky. Presently she faced him again.

'I suppose I ought to thank you for saving my life,' she said.

There was a faint trace of sarcasm in her voice and for a moment it surprised her. She hadn't intended it, but since it had crept into her tone she was quite content to have it there. It was a sort of challenge to him and she wondered how he would react to it.

'Go 'head,' he said coolly.

'Thank you,' she said dryly.

He nodded but said nothing. She eyed him curiously.

'You don't like people, do you?' she asked shortly.

He grinned fleetingly.

'Mebbe they don't like me,' he answered.

'I don't believe many people do,' she said evenly. 'Because I don't think I like you, either.'

He laughed lightly.

'Reckon thet's all right,' he answered calmly. 'Jest b'cause I happened t' come along

110

and hauled you outta thet fire don't mean you gotta like me.'

A frown deepened over her face. She suppressed an urge to shake him.

'Why did you risk your life to save mine?' she demanded.

He shrugged his shoulder.

'Oh, I dunno,' he drawled. 'Mebbe I jest didn't stop t'think 'bout anythin' but gettin' you outta there.'

Her lips thinned scornfully. He slid out of the saddle. He was tall she noted at a glance, well over six feet in height. He was broad-shouldered too with a tapering waistline like an athlete. He moved lightly, panther-like, despite his size. Beneath his tight-fitting shirt she could see muscles ripple and contract. She turned her head quickly when he stepped toward her.

'Reckon we'd better be movin' along,' she heard him say.

She made no answer, made no attempt to rise. She knew instinctively that he was bending over her and she forced herself to keep her eyes averted. His big hands slid under her arms. He lifted her easily to her feet. He turned toward the horse, then he looked back at her.

'Well?' he demanded.

'I'm cold.'

111

He grunted, unstrapped the bulky roll behind the saddle and whipped out a blanket.

'Hyar,' he said gruffly.

The blanket came thudding across space and into her hastily thrown up arms, the blanket slapping harshly against her cheek. She colored, but said nothing. She opened the blanket, draped it around her, then looked up at him quietly. There was a strange, crimson patch on her cheek. He bent swiftly and swept her up in his arms. For a brief moment their eyes met, clashed, then her eyes wavered and fell. He carried her forward to the horse. The big black turned his head and watched with apparent interest. Harris lifted her in the saddle, pushed her booted feet into the stirrups, then he climbed up behind her. His big hands slid around her, reaching for the reins. The horse clattered off presently.

They jogged past the boulder at the top of the trail. She looked up quickly when she heard cries below them. She turned in the saddle, opened her mouth to say something, caught a glimpse of the cold gleam in his eyes. Slowly she turned.

The iron shoes of the horse rang out sharply as he clattered on. They swung over onto a steep, winding trail that led higher into the hills. Once she turned slightly and looked back, then she settled herself more firmly, leaned forward a bit in an effort to avoid leaning against him.

A sharp wind swept down from the snow-capped peaks. She was thankful then for the blanket and buried her chin in its folds. A huge, black-winged bird swooped down out of the sky, wheeled overhead, dove at breakneck speed and swept over them, climbed swiftly and soared away toward the distant peaks.

CHAPTER NINE

It was noon when they made their first halt of consequence. The early morning chill had gone and now the air grew steadily warmer as the sun rose higher in the cloudless sky. Now the sun was directly overhead. Even the rugged hills appeared to welcome it for some of their bleakness and unfriendliness wilted before it. In the distance the sun's bright rays crowned the towering snow-capped peaks that thrust their spires so high into the blue sky; splashed them with brilliant, riotous colors that dazzled the eye. Closer at hand, Carol discovered intermittent patches of grass, but in the main, the hills were desolate and barren.

All through the morning they had ridden in

silence, following first one trail then another, continuing on along the second when the first trail faded out. Now they pulled up in a small boulder-encircled clearing. There was a cluster of small rocks in the middle of the clearing, scorched and smoke-blackened rocks that attested to the fact that someone had built a fire there before. Harris slid to the ground, halted momentarily and looked up at Carol.

'Git down,' he said briefly.

He made no attempt to help her dismount; simply stood by and waited. She gripped the saddle horn and tried to dismount. She found to her complete dismay that she was stiff and cramped. One leg acted as if it had long since lost all power of movement and locomotion. She made another supreme effort, managed to swing the leg clear of the horn, then she lost her grip. She clutched at the horn frantically, missed it, plummeted earthward and came to an abrupt halt in Harris' arms. She gave him an icy glare. He grinned broadly, evidence that he had enjoyed her unusual method of dismounting. He set her down upon the ground. The blanket trailed after her on the ground. He said nothing; merely glanced at it, then at her. She followed his eyes, lifted the blanket, folded it deliberately and dropped it on a tiny patch of grass.

'Wouldn't do that,' he said casually. 'Might

114

find a snake or somethin' curled up in it the next time you use it. Kinda annoyin', y'know, 'specially when you aint hankerin' fer company.'

She flushed, bent quickly despite painful protestations from her awakening muscles, picked up the blanket and held it firmly in her arms. She turned her head deliberately to avoid meeting his eyes. When he turned his back, she turned again also, slowly, watched as he unsaddled his horse.

'Cain't offer you nuthin' better'n a rock t'sit on,' he said presently over his shoulder. 'Reckon you kin take yo' pick, though. Lots of 'em aroun'.'

She looked about her. Just beyond her was a small square rock with a smooth surface. She marched over to it, seated herself and looked up. He glanced at her fleetingly, then dropped the saddle on the ground and followed it with the saddle bags. Impatience showed in her face.

'I don't suppose,' she began in icy tones, 'that it has occurred to you that I might be hungry?'

'Oh,' he answered lightly without looking at her, 'it might have.'

She glared at him but said nothing for a moment.

'I don't know what your usual practice is,'

she began again shortly, 'but do you usually feed the women you kidnap, or do you starve them into submission?'

He gave her a side-long glance.

'Ain't never done no kidnapping',' he said presently. 'Cain't jest tell what I'd do till I've tried it.'

She looked up with widening eyes.

'Then I'm not being kidnapped?'

He shook his head very gravely.

'Nope.'

She sat silent for a minute.

'I'm almost disappointed now. You aren't particularly sociable or even interesting, not even in your best he-man way, and now that the thrill of the kidnapping is gone, I'm afraid you're going to be very boring,' she said. He patted the big black's sleek neck.

'Thet so?'

'Of course.' She watched him for a moment in silence. 'Why are we here and where are we going?'

'We're headin' back,' he said simply. 'On'y we're agoin' thetaway,' nodding toward the hills that still lay ahead of them, ''stead o' th' way we come.'

She followed his eyes for a moment, frowned and turned again to face him. It was obvious from the frown that she didn't understand.

'But why can't we go back,' she demanded, turning and nodding as he had done, in the direction of the prairie land from which they had come, 'thetaway?'

She smiled brazenly now, tauntingly, as she mimicked him. If he noticed it, he gave no sign. She watched him, curious to see his reaction.

'Ain't no way outa here,' he answered presently. 'Leastways, not that way.'

He pronounced the last two words carefully and nodded again, but this time toward the route which they had followed. She permitted a smile to show on her face for she was anxious to let him know that she had enjoyed making him correct his speech.

'But there was a way in, wasn't there?' she continued.

He nodded briefly.

'Same's the way out, on'y I blowed it clean t'hell and back again,' he explained with surprising patience. 'Soon's them raiders got through th' pass, I blowed it up.'

Her eyes opened wide.

'The raiders? You mean . . . they're here?' she asked quickly, concern in her voice and face.

It was his turn to smile now and smile he did, tauntingly as she had done, and exasperatingly, too. He wanted her to know

117

that he was enjoying something at her expense, even though it was only the alarm she felt.

'What'll we do?' she asked, looking about her anxiously.

'Do?' he laughed lightly. 'I dunno. You got some ideas?'

She flashed him a murderous look.

'Reckon I'll jest fix me a little somethin' t' eat while you figger out somethin' we kin do,' he said. 'Don't suppose you feel much like eatin' now, eh? Might interfere with yo' thinkin'.' He gave her a side-long glance. 'You jest set thar and do all the thinkin' you want. When you hit on somethin' you jest holler.'

She closed her jaws with a snap. He stole a look at her and grinned to himself. He busied himself making a small fire. One of his saddle bags yielded a battered coffee pot and a few other pans considerably the worse for use and wear. She turned away, but minutes later the strong aroma of freshly made coffee and frying bacon assailed her. Reluctantly she turned. She stared at him. Presently the stares became a baleful glare. He was nibbling a piece of bacon and wielding a cup of coffee with evident enjoyment. He looked up at her.

'Think o' somethin'?' he asked.

'No!' she snapped.

He looked at her with an air of surprise and

innocence.

'Mebbe you ain't concentratin',' he said shortly. He swallowed a mouthful of coffee. There was a pan of sizzling bacon within reach. He lifted a piece of bacon with his fingers, gingerly, chewed it slowly, smacked his lips as he downed it. 'Uh-m-m,' he said, half aloud. 'Thet's good. Yes sir, mighty good.'

He reached for the battered coffee pot and poured himself another cupful. He shifted himself, stretched his long legs, sighed and lay back against a rock. Slowly he drank his coffee, put down the cup and rolled a cigarette. He dug in his pockets for a match, found one and scratched it on a rock, lit the cigarette and inhaled deeply. He sent a thin stream of smoke skyward. He picked up the cup again, drank from it slowly, then put it down again. Presently he looked at her.

'Doin' any better now?' he asked.

'No!' she snapped coldly.

He shrugged his shoulder.

'Shucks,' he said presently. 'You ain't half tryin'.'

He looked at her again, questioningly.

'Reckon some bacon and coffee'd help any?' he asked innocently.

'What do you think?' she asked coldly.

He shrugged his shoulder.

'Dunno. 'Course some folks cain't do more'n one thing et a time, y'know, an' do thet proper. An' when it comes t'doing more, like eatin' and singin', mebbe eatin' an' thinkin', too, why, doggone ef they ain't licked 'fore they begin.' He paused and eyed her for a moment. 'Still, ef you wanna take a chance, heck, I ain't th' one t'object.'

'You're certain you won't miss some of that bacon and coffee?' she asked politely. 'I wouldn't think of depriving you of anything, you know, for the world.'

'Heck,' he said. 'Feller cain't eat more'n his fill, kin he? Jest help y'self.'

'Thank you,' she said with forced sweetness.

'That's all right. Share an' share alike, I allus say. Go 'head,' he concluded.

He drew his hat down over his eyes, stretched his legs again and sighed audibly. He heard her step, heard her rattle the coffee pot. Perhaps the faintest shadow of a grin swept over his mouth.

'The coffee,' he heard her say in a surprised tone.

'Whut's the matter with it?' he asked without moving.

'There . . . there isn't any more.'

'Heck,' he said, turning slightly. 'Don't tell me I drunk it all?'

120

'You know you did,' she said angrily. 'Why you contemptible . . .'

'Whoa,' he said quickly, interrupting her. He struggled into a sitting position, shoved his hat back on his head and looked at her reproachfully. 'Now ain't thet jest like a woman?' He shook his head sadly. 'Callin' a feller names when he's jest tryin' t'do a good turn.' He shook his head again. ''Tain't right.'

She eyed him coldly. Her lips thinned into a straight line. She looked down at the battered coffee pot in her hand. A strange light flashed into her eyes.

'Now, now,' he said hastily. 'Don't go gittin' ideas. 'Tain't lady-like, y'know.'

She frowned, lowered the pot a bit, slowly, almost reluctantly. He watched her carefully.

'A feller cain't be 'spected t'measure whut he eats an' drinks, kin he?' he asked.

The coffee pot came down fully. He relaxed and sank back against the rock again.

'Now ef you look in one o' them thar bags, like's not you'll find s'more coffee,' he said shortly.

'And water for the coffee?' she asked sweetly. 'Will I find that in a bag, too?'

'Heck, no,' he said quickly. 'Reckon that oughta be a canteen around someplace. You jest hunt aroun' fer it. Boun' t' turn up, y'know.'

She gave him an icy stare, turned away and bent over the saddle bags grouped beyond the fire. The big black horse halted his nibbling at a nearby patch of grass and looked up at her for a moment, then he went on again. Harris flipped his cigarette butt away, pulled his hat down over his eyes, slid down again, full length, sighed and finally lay still. Once or twice Carol turned and glanced at him contemptuously. Minutes later she strode over and halted beside him.

'Wake up,' she commanded.

He grunted and stirred slightly. She drove her boot into his ribs.

'Hey!' he yelled. He sat upright, shoved his hat back and looked up at her. 'What th' heck's th' idea kickin' a feller, huh?'

She looked at him wide-eyed, innocence on her face.

'Why, you must be mistaken,' she said quickly, reproachfully. 'You don't think I'd kick you, do you?'

He rubbed his ribs tenderly.

'Well,' he said slowly, 'I dunno. Mebbe I was dreamin'.'

'Of course you were,' she said.

She bent over him.

'The canteen,' she said sweetly. 'Remember it?'

'Shore. Why?'

She scowled fiercely.

'Where is it?' she demanded.

He looked quickly on either side of him, looked up at her and shook his head, then he slid his hand under him. He raised his head slowly and grinned sheepishly.

'Doggone it,' he said lamely. 'Now how d'ya s'pose it got thar?'

She gave him an icy stare.

'I wonder,' she said coldly.

He handed her the canteen. She took it without comment, turned on her heel and marched back to the fire. He grinned again and slowly sank down again. He turned on his side and watched her for a minute.

'Hey,' he called.

She gave no sign that she had heard him.

'Hey,' he called again, louder.

She turned slowly and looked over at him.

'When thet coffee's ready,' he said, 'pour me some, willya?'

She smiled lightly.

'I'll be glad to,' she answered.

He eyed her questioningly for a moment, rubbed his chin reflectively, looked sharply at her again and frowned. He wondered if he had heard her correctly. He couldn't understand the sudden change in her manner. Her eyes were heavy, so he simply decided he'd have to shut them and sleep on it. Minutes later she bent over him. He opened his eyes with a start, looking up at her and grinned.

'Been sleepin' with one eye open,' he said shortly. 'Been wonderin' ef thet thar ghost was aimin' t'kick me in th' ribs again.'

She smiled fleetingly.

'Silly,' she said. 'Shall I pour you some coffee?'

'Huh? Oh, shore, go 'head.'

The smile deepened over her face.

'There's only one cup, you know,' she said.

'On'y one, eh? Well, you use it,' he answered.

'Thank you. I was hoping you'd say that. In fact I've been praying for it. Well, here's your coffee,' she said pleasantly.

The battered coffee pot suddenly appeared from behind her. His eyes opened wide. He sensed what was coming and tried to roll out of range. The coffee followed and overtook him. He bellowed and sputtered, struggled to his knees, clutched at the dripping seat of his pants with both hands and fled, leaving a liquid trail behind him.

CHAPTER TEN

Sunset over the hills, a riot of dazzling, awing colors, of scarlet and purple and gold flooding the western sky. The towering peaks now not so distant reared their lofty spires high into the brilliantly hued sky. Below them the ragged hills glowed darkly. Far below the hills lay the rolling, far-stretching prairie-land. In the sunset and gathering dusk it gave the appearance of a huge, limitless but somewhat wrinkled green carpet.

Presently the flaming colors faded above the towering snow-capped peaks. A robe of purple shadows swathed them and dusk spread its mantle over the hills. Here and there in the darkening sky a tiny, twinkling, silvery star broke through the blue canopy. With evening came a stiff breeze, drifting southward from the snowy peaks. Silent almost as the breeze, a troop of lengthening shadows slipped down and blacked out the earth.

Below, in the distant prairie land, a lonely coyote wailed plaintively. From the hills a voice answered, the snarling tone of a timber wolf, gray by day and black by night, calling to the pack that had gone on without him.

Now a third voice took up the cry; the deep-throated, growling voice of a mountain lion. The far-away coyote heard it and bounded away. The timber wolf heard the lion's cry too, turned and slunk away in the shadows. The lion growled again presently, then it wheeled slowly and jogged off on padded feet. It was night now, night over the hills.

A gray-black figure bounded across the trail, snarled and leaped. The big black horse shied, reared, pawed madly with its fore feet. The girl cried out in terror. A Colt roared and flamed. The wolf screamed, bounded high in the air, spun crazily for a moment, then it crashed just beyond the trail and lay still, a motionless and grotesquely sprawled figure with a cruel mouth that gaped strangely.

'Easy,' the man said presently, reassuringly.

The big black subsided and went on again, gingerly and on the alert, instinctively skirted the body of the wolf that lay close by. Perhaps the horse quickened his pace a bit too. The man's hand gripped the shoulder of the girl in front of him.

'Jest a wolf,' he said casually. He turned in his saddle and looked down at the dead beast. 'Big feller,' he said briefly.

The girl laughed nervously.

'For a moment I thought it was a lion,' she

126

said.

'You'd aknowed it ef it was,' he answered.

They went on again in silence. The girl raised her head and looked up at the sky then at the shadowy peaks ahead. She glanced fleetingly too at the black rims of the hills, drew the blanket closer about her, buried her chin in its folds and settled back. Now she made no effort to lean forward, to keep her distance from the man who rode behind her on the saddle. His proximity seemed to give her a sense of security and she was thankful for it.

'Ned,' she said suddenly.

It was the first time she had called him that.

'Yeah?'

'I'm trying to think of you as Marshall,' she said slowly. 'Picturing you as I saw you that day in Red Dog.'

'In Red Dog, eh?'

'Yes,' she went on. 'In the bank the day you ... well, the day it was held up.'

He made no answer, waited for her to continue.

'I was there, you know,' she said gently.

'Redburn was thar, too.'

'Yes, I know that.'

'Well?'

'Somehow,' she began again, 'I can't believe it was really you that I saw there. You were so different. You weren't Ned Harris that day. You were a stranger, a man named Marshall, a man who took another's life with such little concern that I shudder when I think of it.' She was silent for a moment. 'I'm glad it was Marshall who did that. I'm trying to forget what he looked like. I'm telling myself that it wasn't you but that it was a man I'd never seen before, one that I'll never see again, I hope.' She laughed.

'Why?' he asked in a strange and hollow voice. 'Why yuh doin thet?'

'I don't know,' she said slowly. 'It's something I can feel but can't explain. Does that make sense to you?'

'Dunno,' he answered briefly.

He halted the big black. He slid to the ground, turned and held out his arms to her. He stood still, waiting, looking up at her. The moonlight suddenly lighted his face, framed it against his black garb and the shadows. She turned and swung one leg over the saddle horn, slid down into his waiting arms.

'Girl,' he whispered.

His big hands slid over her slim shoulders, tightened, then suddenly crushed her to him. His eager lips sought and found hers, crushed them too. The blanket fell away. Her arms came up slowly, over his chest and up around his neck. She clung to him, straightened up

128

against him. The shadowy hills, the moon and the stars spun wildly about her. She lost track of time, forgot everything in that brief moment; when he released her, she was breathless. He stepped past her toward the idling horse, fumbled with the straps behind the saddle, yanked off the bulky roll and dropped it to the ground. She looked up at him curiously expectantly, wondering what he would say, wondering if he would say anything. Her fingers strayed to her bruised, tingling lips. It was a mechanical movement and one that she didn't even notice.

'Reckon you'd better turn in,' he said shortly without looking at her. His voice was different, husky and emotional.

He opened the roll, dragged it across the trail, spread it open full length close to a huge boulder with a strange, white, sun-bleached face. He straightened up, rode past her again, loosened the cinches beneath the big black's belly, removed the saddle and carried it to the other side of the trail and put it down. He picked up the blanket that she had dropped and forgotten and tossed it on top of the saddle. He took the bridle and led the big black away. She turned slowly and looked after him, until he faded out in the darkness. Then she heard his voice somewhere beyond her, heard him talk to the horse, heard the horse's answering neigh. Slowly she trudged toward the open bed roll. A double blanket awaited her. She dropped down, gathering the blanket about her, stretched out and turned on her side toward the white-faced boulder. Minutes later she heard his step.

She lay still, waiting again, wondering too if now he would say something. But the minutes passed and still he made no attempt to come to her. She turned and looked across the trail. She saw him standing there, a tall, dark figure, looking toward the tall peaks. There was a cigarette in his hand, and a thin wisp of smoke curled lightly up the length of his arm. When he lifted the cigarette to his lips it flamed brilliantly for a moment, lighting up his face. She wondered what he was thinking, wondered too if he was trying to reconstruct in his mind as she was doing in hers, the event that now seemed so blurred and so impossible.

There was no explaining what had happened. He had caught her to him and she had yielded without hesitation. There had been no warning, nothing but the fact that he had communicated his passion and longing to her and she had responded. Strangely too, she felt no remorse.

In the darkness now she could see little of his face. Womanlike she had to know what he was thinking, how he would attempt, if he did at all, to explain what had happened.

'Ned,' she called softly.

He turned slowly and looked over at her.

'Ned,' she called again.

He tossed the cigarette away and strode over. In the darkness he loomed even taller than otherwise.

'Ned,' she began, looking up at him. 'What were you thinking about?

'You,' he answered simply.

His probing eyes swept her face. In the darkness she thought she detected a twitching of the muscles of his lean jaws. His answer was all she had hoped for, but now that he had given it, she wanted to hear more, wanted to peer deeper into this strange man.

'Bend down, please,' she said shortly. 'I want to look at you.'

He dropped to one knee beside her, knelt there quietly while she looked hard at him.

'Why did you kiss me?' she asked.

He shrugged his shoulder.

'Dunno. Reckon I jest wanted to, an' well, I did. Thet's all,' he said slowly.

'And now,' she pressed, 'you're sorry?'

'Some.'

'Why?' she asked curiously.

He was silent for a moment.

'Reckon I had no right to,' he said quietly. 'I'm askin' yo' pardon.'

131

He came erect swiftly, turned on his heel and strode away. For a while she lay still, looking up at the blue sky with unseeing eyes. She glanced across the trail. He had rolled himself in the single blanket and now he lay still, flat on his broad back, staring skyward as she had done. Slowly she settled back. Presently she closed her eyes.

In her dreams he reappeared. It was in the bank at Red Dog. She saw him plainly; a tall, black-clad man with a lean, tensed face and steely eyes, and a heavy, smoking Colt in his steady hand. She shook her head, trying to force the vision from her mind. Presently, it faded away. There was a brief interlude, then he reappeared. But now there was something different about him. As before he was tall and of course, black-clad. His face was calm and relaxed and the frightening tenseness had vanished. Then too his eyes were clear and for the moment, strangely soft. There was nothing steely or awing about them now. There was no smoking, death-dealing Colt in his hand; instead his guns hung low against his muscular thighs. He smiled fleetingly, bared his even, white teeth. She heard his voice, the drawling tone that grew on one. Then he was pressing her to him. She felt his starved, eager lips on hers. In her sleep she smiled, settled a bit deeper in the blankets.

Then with startling suddenness it was dawn, a gray, misty, damp dawn that hung like a pall over the drab hills. Then she felt a strange sensation, suddenly realized that someone was shaking her. She opened her eyes. Ned Harris was bending over her.

'Reckon you'd better git up,' she heard him say. 'We're gittin' company.'

'Company?' she repeated. For a moment she was puzzled, then she grasped the full significance of his remark. She looked at him quickly, questioningly and anxiously.

'Who . . . who is it? she asked.

'Dunno fer sure,' he said.

She cast the blankets aside and got to her feet. She glanced at the trail nervously.

'Now don't git t' worryin',' he said, following her eyes. 'Ef it's th' fellers I'm thinkin' they are, I reckon they'll be peaceable. Ef it ain't, well . . .' his voice trailed away.

'What do you want me to do?' she asked.

'Nuthin' much,' he answered. 'Jest keep back a piece, see? I'll do th' talkin' or whatever else I figger's needed.'

There was again a grim significance to his words. He loosened the Colts in their holsters. Anxiety showed in her eyes.

'Jest in case,' he said lightly, patting the guns.

'You'll be careful, won't you?' she asked.

He smiled fleetingly.

''Course,' he answered.

He turned and strolled forward, halted and retraced his steps. She looked up.

'Thar's somethin' else,' he said simply.

'Yes?'

'Some fellers git mighty careless when they git a gun in thar han's,' he said quietly. 'Ef thar's any signs o' gunplay, git under cover in a hurry. Don't fergit.'

He turned on his heel and strode off. She looked after him, marveled at his manner. Suddenly she realized that she was unusually calm and unafraid. Again he had communicated his feeling to her and quite unconsciously she had responded. In a material and tangible way, she felt completely confident of the outcome; for watching him, just knowing that he was there, gave her all the assurance she needed. Now she heard horses' hoofs, heard the approaching ring of iron shoes on rock. Harris turned and glanced at her. She gave him a fleeting smile. He nodded and went on again, halted at the head of the trail.

There were two huge bald-faced boulders forming a sort of gateway at the head of the trail, one on either side. Presently the head and shoulders of a bullet-headed, swarthy

134

man appeared between the boulders. He halted his horse, looked questioningly and appraisingly at Harris, then he caught a glimpse of Carol. For a moment he looked sharply at her, his beady eyes sweeping her, then he looked down again at Harris. Another horseman pulled up behind the first man, then two other mounted men filled the passageway. The last man in line stood up in his stirrups and looked at Harris.

'Howdy,' the swarthy man said.

Harris nodded briefly.

'Howdy,' he said.

He had halted in the middle of the trail, his hands resting upon the butts of his Colts.

'Passin' through?' he asked casually.

'Nope. Lookin' fer a feller an' a girl,' the man answered quietly.

'Thet so? Whut kinda feller?'

The swarthy man grinned.

'Ain't quite sure,' he answered. 'Didn't git close nuff t' see, but I'd say he was a big feller, jest 'bout yo' size an' build.'

'Uh-huh. Anythin' else?'

'Wa-al,' the man continued, 'I ain't whut you'd call positive 'bout it, but I kinda got'n idea he was wearin' dark clo'es an' thet he was ridin' a black hoss.'

'H'm,' Harris said briefly. 'Go on, stranger.'

135

'Then,' the man went on presently, 'It looked t' me like there was a girl ridin' in front o' him.' His beady eyes strayed over toward Carol. 'Looked somethin' like her.'

Harris made no comment. The swarthy man turned in his saddle, nodded to the men behind him, then he looked at Harris again.

'Mister,' he said shortly. 'Whut color hoss you ridin'?'

Harris grinned.

'A black un,' he said quietly.

The swarthy man smiled.

'Thet so?' he mused. 'Wearin' black clo'es an' ridin' a black hoss, eh? Funny, ain't it?'

'Mebbe. Anythin' else, Hawkins?'

The swarthy man looked hard at him for a moment. A frown swept his face.

'How'd yuh know m' name?' he demanded.

Harris laughed lightly.

'Reckon most everybody knows Hawkins' Raiders,' he said. 'Some even know Hawkins.'

The swarthy man eyed him.

'Whut's yo' name, Mister?' he asked shortly.

'Marshall. Ever hear it b'fore?'

The man smiled lightly.

'Mebbe' He glanced at Carol again. 'That Fred Hall's girl?'

'Yep. Why?'

The man smiled again.

136

'Reckon I don't hev t' look no further,' he said. 'I'll take thet map now.'

'Map? Whut map?'

Hawkins laughed loudly.

'Whut map, hey?' He roared with laughter. 'Kinda cagey, ain'tcha?'

Harris shrugged his shoulder.

'Mebbe. Whut's this map you're talkin' 'bout?' he asked.

Hawkins stared at him scornfully.

'Yuh wouldn't know, wouldja?' he sneered. 'Hall's girl wit' yuh an' yuh askin' me whut map?' A scowl spred over his face. 'Th' map t' her ol' man's mine,' he snapped.

'Oh, thet map.'

'So now yuh know whut I'm talkin' 'bout eh? Hand it over,' Hawkins commanded.

'Mebbe I aim t' use it,' Harris said quietly.

The swarthy man's eyes blazed.

'Mister,' he said coldly, 'I'm in a hurry, see?'

Harris smiled fleetingly.

'Y'know,' he mused. 'Thar was a feller over t' Yuma once, a hairy feller an' yo' spittin' image, too, Hawkins. An' now thet I think o' it, his name was Hawkins. Clem Hawkins, I think 'twas.'

'Go on, Mister,' Hawkins said. 'I'm plumb int'rested.'

'Wa-al,' Harris went on, 'this Hawkins

137

feller, this Clem, was allus in a hurry. When he started t'do somethin', he wouldn't let nuthin' interfere wit' whut he aimed t'do. He got a notion one day thet he didn't like Yuma. 'Course he coulda pulled up stakes an' hightailed fer other parts, but thet wasn't his way o' doin' things.'

'Git t'th' point,' Hawkins said impatiently.

'Ain't much more t' th' yarn,' Ned said in answer. 'Anyway, Clem got purty well lickered up one day an' set out t' burn down the town. He come bustin' into a saloon an' foun' a feller leanin' over th' bar pourin' himself a drink. Clem hung aroun' a minute an' when he figgered the feller was takin' a heap sight too much time in downin' his drink, he jest upped an' shot th' glass outta the feller's han'.'

'Yuh don' say?'

'I shore do. Wa-al, th' feller jest pulled his own gun an' drilled Clem. They planted Clem th' next day an' nobody else has ever tried t' burn down Yuma since. It was jest too bad, but it musta taught Clem a lesson thet it don't allus pay t' do things too fast. There's allus some folks thet don't like t' be rushed.'

'I hadda brother named Clem,' Hawkins said presently.

'Thet so? Then this feller I been tellin' yuh 'bout mighta been him, eh?'

138

'Mebbe.'

There was a strange silence for a minute, then one of the waiting horsemen urged his mount forward a bit, leaned forward in his saddle and nudged Hawkins. The bullet-headed man turned. The horseman simply nodded to Hawkins. The latter gripped his horse's reins, backed his mount slowly. Already the other horsemen had swung around and now Harris could hear their horses' hoofs as they disappeared from view.

'So long, Mister,' Hawkins said.

'Adios,' Harris answered.

Hawkins spurred his horse. In a moment he had gone. In the distance the clatter of galloping horses died down, presently it faded out completely. Harris frowned.

'Funny,' he muttered to himself. 'Never 'spected thet hellion'd back water without puttin' up somethin' uva fight.'

He rubbed his chin reflectively for a moment, then he shrugged his shoulder, turned slowly and trudged back to Carol's side. He looked up, stared and halted. There was no sign of her. He dashed forward.

'Carol,' he called.

She had probably taken cover during his conversation with Hawkins. That was it. She'd pop up in a minute from behind one of the boulders.

'Carol,' he called again.

Still there was no answer. A frown clouded his face. He dashed from boulder to boulder but there was no sign of her. He halted and studied the ground but there was nothing there to indicate that she had fled. Rocks bore no testimony of footprints. His eyes glinted dangerously. Then suddenly he gasped.

'Doggone,' he muttered. 'Thar were six men this mornin' an' now thar were only four. Two uv 'em musta circled aroun' while Hawkins an' I were palaverin' and got away wit' her. No wonder that coyote backed down.'

He was silent for a moment, then he nodded vigorously.

'Sure,' he mumbled bitterly, half aloud. 'Thet was it. Hawkins was willin' t' talk so's, t' give his men time to git th' girl and hightail.'

He cursed roundly. He whistled shrilly, then impatiently a second time. He heard a horse's whinny, then the big black trotted into view. Harris dashed forward. He made no attempt to gather up the roll or the blanket which he had used, simply vaulted into the saddle and sped down the trail which Hawkins and his men had taken.

CHAPTER ELEVEN

All through the long morning Ned Harris clung doggedly to the trail of Hawkins and his men. It had proved a simple matter to pick up their trail following their strange departure and now it would have been just as simple to give the big black his head and permit him to close up the gap between them. However, Ned dared not let them know how close he actually was. Certainly, he reasoned, they expected him to follow once he discovered that Carol Hall had disappeared. It was just as obvious that they knew that he would not accept her disappearance as an accident or that she had slipped away, but that he would immediately connect them with it.

He had long since decided that his only chance of rescuing her from Hawkins lay in following him to his rendezvous with the men who had spirited her away. Accordingly, Ned held back. When Hawkins' men halted for a brief respite, he did, too. When they went on again, he went on, but always he managed to keep out of sight, threading his way behind the protecting screen of boulders that dotted the trail and countryside.

He realized too that they had no intention of

leading him directly to their rendezvous. Once darkness came on and made the going more difficult, they would see to it that they succeeded in 'shaking' him. Of course, the many ravines and gulleys in the hills made an ambush a constant threat, and one which he would have to guard against. Then, too, between the hills and the mountains wound many small but swift-flowing streams. Somewhere along their banks Hawkins would see to it that they lost him or drove him off. Grimly he acknowledged those facts but he told himself that he would have to chance them.

At noon the sun was brightest and directly overhead. As time went on, it drifted lazily toward the West, over the towering spires of the peaks. Presently it was late afternoon and from the snow-capped peaks stiff winds swept southward. Now the hills grew sullen and drab and bleak and the tall peaks looked black and cold. Dusk came on swiftly, shrouding the peaks in shadows. Even the rugged lips of the hills faded and merged with the shadows. The sun cast purplish rays over the snow in the distance and as it hung low over the rim of the hills it flooded the sky with dazzling colors.

The big black grew more restless and he stamped impatiently as the sharp wind swept past. He was anxious to move faster, anxious to run. He champed at the bit and fought continually for his head. He snorted angrily, impatiently, and pawed the hard ground whenever there was a halt, even a brief one. It was with difficulty that Ned held him down. More than once he tugged savagely at the reins and spoke sharply to the horse.

They topped a low rise, and a narrow flat land through which a little river flowed like a ribbon of silver. There was thick brush and sage on the distant bank of the river. Also there were tall, broad-trunked trees beyond them. Ned halted and watched as the four men forded the river and emerged on the opposite bank. He noted that two of the men dismounted while the burly Hawkins galloped off through the brush and trees. The fourth man lagged behind for a minute then he rode off after Hawkins. The two who had dismounted led their horses into the brush. Presently they disappeared from view. Ned laughed lightly. This was to be the first attempt to halt him. All he had to do to accommodate the waiting men was to ford the river so that they could shoot him down from their places of concealment.

Ned Harris was too old a hand at such a game. He would cross the river under cover of darkness, then all things would be equal. He turned for a moment and studied a rising and falling black smudge in the distance. It was, he soon decided, a single rider. He watched the approaching rider curiously. The pressure of his heavy Winchester in the saddleboot beneath his right knee was comforting, particularly since he could see the butt of a rifle protruding from the newcomer's saddle. Ned leaned over and loosened the rifle in its leather sheath. On and on came the lone rider, growing larger and larger in the fast-fading light.

Ned noted a faltering irregularity in the approaching horse's hoof beats. 'Horse's jest 'bout all in,' he told himself. 'He'll be blamed lucky ef he makes it t' th' top o' th' rise.'

The horse faltered. Ned saw him look up in the dusk, saw him stumble drunkenly to within fifty feet of where he himself waited in the protecting shadow of a bounder. Down went the horse, hurling his rider over his head. The horse struggled to his feet almost instantly and stood quivering, with legs shaky and wide spread and head hanging. The rider lay still for a moment, groaned and rolled over.

Harris swung out of the saddle and raced toward the prostrate man. He saw the man struggle to his knees, saw a shifting glint of metal in the man's hand. Ned sidestepped nimbly and launched a prodigious kick. His boot toe caught the fallen man's wrist and sent the gun spinning from his hand. He bent swiftly, grabbed the man's shirt collar and jerked him to his feet. He whipped out a heavy Colt and jammed it into the man's ribs. Ned looked sharply at the man, then he laughed.

'Huh, so it's you, eh, Jenkins?'

Smith Jenkins massaged his right arm tenderly. Ned noted that an empty sling hung from the youthful ranger's neck.

'Been wonderin' when'n hell you'd be showin' up,' he said briefly. 'Gen'lly you're so close behin' me, I kin almost feel yo' breath on my neck.'

Jenkins went on rubbing his injured arm. Finally he slipped it into the sling and held the arm close to his body. Presently he stopped rubbing it and looked up.

'Where's th' girl?' he demanded.

Harris laughed lightly.

'Ne'er mind th' girl now, Mister,' he said coldly. 'Reckon it's 'bout time you an' me settled somethin' thet's been hanging' fire fer a long time. Mebbe I oughta blast you while I got th' chance. An' don't make no move fer thet other gun yuh got, understan'? Mebbe I'd better take it b'fore yuh gits foolish 'bout it.'

He leaned forward and yanked out the gun

145

that hung at Jenkins' left side. He jammed it into his belt. He backed away from the ranger, slowly, retreating toward the spot where he had sent Jenkins' gun spinning. Presently he reached it, bent swiftly without taking his eyes from his captive, snapped up the gun and shoved it into his belt too. Then he sauntered forward again.

'Wa-al, Mister,' he began, 'ef yuh got somethin' t' say, say it.'

Jenkins grinned coldly.

'You wouldn't believe it, Harris,' he said scornfully. 'So shoot an' be damned.'

Ned laughed.

'Kinda anxious t' git it over wit', ain't cha? I got time,' he said. He glanced skyward fleetingly. 'I kin wait 'til dark. Go 'head. Talk.'

The ranger shook his head doggedly.

'Not 'til I know about Carol Hall,' he said. 'What've yuh done with 'er?'

Harris' eyes glinted momentarily.

'Whut makes yuh so sure I know anythin' 'bout th' girl?' he asked curiously.

Jenkins snorted.

'Quit stallin',' he said scornfully. 'I know yuh got 'er outta th' fire. I spotted yo' tracks back o' th' barn an' followed yuh since. What's more, I could tell from yo' horse's tracks that he was carryin' double. So I know
146

she was wit' yuh. I'd gotten yuh sooner, on'y that damned bridge yuh blew up, made me circle aroun' fed a couple of hours 'till I foun' 'nother way inter th' hills.'

'Purty smart, eh?' Ned paused for a moment. 'I know yuh won't believe it,' he said slowly, 'but Hawkins got 'er.

Jenkins gasped. He stared at Harris.

'Hawkins?' he repeated. 'How?'

'Stole 'er when I wasn't watchin',' he answered quietly.

The ranger's eyes flashed.

'You're a liar, Harris,' he cried hotly. 'An' yuh know it.' Contempt blazed into his face and voice. 'Stole 'er!' he laughed scornfully. 'Like's not yuh handed 'er over t' that skunk!'

The heavy Colt in Ned Harris' hand leaped upward.

'Mister,' he said deliberately. 'One more crack like thet one an' I'll blow yuh apart.'

Jenkins grinned fleetingly.

'Yuh ain't got th' nerve t' do it,' he said coldly. 'Anyway, if what yuh say is true, how come yuh ain't tailin' that butcher? Don't tell me yuh ain't no better'n that hellion?'

Ned Harris eyed him for a moment, then he pointed to the narrow ribbon of shimmering silver below them.

'See thet river down thar, Jenkins?' he asked.

147

The ranger turned slowly and followed Ned's pointing finger.

'What 'bout it?' he demanded.

'See thet clump o' brush an' trees, jest beyon' th' river bank?' Harris asked. Jenkins looked as directed. He gazed again at the river, then at the brush and trees. 'Jest behin' 'em are two o' Hawkins' men. Thar waitin' fer me, waitin' t' plug me th' minute I come across th' river.' He was silent for a moment. 'I'm goin' across when it gits good'n dark. Does thet satisfy you, Jenkins?'

'Mebbe,' the ranger said slowly. Then turning to face Harris again, 'It's purty dark now, ain't it? Git goin' b'fore they do.'

Harris laughed softly and shook his head.

'Reckon they'll wait 'till I come fer 'em. B'sides, I still got some bus'ness right hyar thet needs 'tendin' to,' he said significantly. He paused for a moment. 'Thought yuh had somethin' t' say, Mister?'

'If it'll make you move faster,' Jenkins said briefly, 'I'll say it. You're all wrong 'bout my dad flimflammin' yo' old man outta his ranch, Harris. It weren't him that done it, but th' fellers that owned th' bank. My dad only worked fer 'em.'

Ned snorted contemptuously.

'On'y worked fer 'em?' he repeated loudly. 'Hell, Ranger, it was him thet got th' ol' man

148

t' sign them papers an' him thet come an' tol' us t' git. Thet's all I gotta know an' all I wanna know,' he concluded bitterly.

Jenkins turned away.

'What's the use?' he said disgustedly. 'You're too doggoned pigheaded t' understan' an' yuh won't.'

Harris made no answer. He turned slowly and gazed at the river below. Now it was more silvery than before, a thin, glistening ribbon that spread away as far as the eye could see. Now darkness was upon them with a sudden sweep that blanketed the entire countryside. He looked up slowly. The nearby peaks loomed up like cathedral spires, rearing their needle-pointed tips into the blue sky above. The surrounding hills were cast in black, solid masses of blackness that were totally devoid of shadow and movement.

'Well?' he heard Jenkins demand impatiently. 'Do somethin', willya? Kill me if you like, or take me wit' yuh.' He paused and pondered for a moment. 'How many in Hawkins' outfit?'

'Six th' first time I seen 'em, when they follered me inter th' hills,' Harris answered. 'Thar weren't but four th' next time I seen 'em. I figger two uv 'em circled aroun' where me an' Hawkins was palaverin' and made off wit' th' girl. Reckon all six o' them'll be together when I ketch up with 'em.'

'Six, huh? Yuh won't have a chance wit' that many, Harris,' the ranger quickly pointed out. 'Lemme go wit' yuh, then if they git one o' us, the other one kin still do somethin'.'

Ned considered for a moment, then he drew Jenkins' guns from his belt and held them out to him. A grin spread over the ranger's face. He took the guns, gladly, shoved them into his holsters. He turned quickly, and whistled to his horse.

'Wait a minute,' Harris said curtly.

Jenkins turned, questioningly.

'Reckon thet one arm o' yourn wouldn't be much uva help in a fight,' Harris said briefly. 'You stay hyar. Ef I don't come back, then yuh kin foller me across.'

'Like hell,' Jenkins said clearly. 'I'm jest as good a man wit' one arm as you are wit' two.'

The roan cantered up. The ranger gripped the reins and vaulted into the saddle.

'Thar's one more thing, Mister,' Harris said. 'Ef they don't git us, when this thing is over, I still aim to settle thet bus'ness between us. I ain't fergittin' it, savvy?'

Jenkins laughed lightly.

'You're a damned fool, Harris, an' allus will be, I reckon,' he said lightly. 'Shake a leg.'

Harris strode back to where the big black horse was nibbling at some grass. Jenkins followed at his heels. Ned mounted, wheeled and galloped off toward the river. The roan, now rested, pranced lightly to the water's edge, shied and held back. The ranger dug his spurs into his mount's flanks. The roan plunged into the water, shooting spray high into the air. Harris' horse stepped forward, treading the cold water gingerly. Together they went on. Midway, the current ran swiftest. The roan lost his footing and stumbled awkwardly. Frantically, Jenkins strove to bring him erect. The big black wheeled alongside. Harris leaned forward in the saddle, grabbed the bridle and jerked the roan to his feet, then they went on again. Minutes later they clambered up the bank.

'This way,' Ned called, swerving away from the point at which he had seen Hawkins' men enter the brush.

'Right behin' yuh,' the ranger answered.

They galloped on a way, then Harris pulled up and dismounted. Jenkins reined in presently and slid out of the saddle.

'Aim t' go on afoot?' he asked.

'Figger it'll be a heap easier trailin' them two fellers into th' brush afoot,' Ned replied. 'When we finish with' 'em, we'll come back fer th' horses an' go on.'

'Right.'

With Harris in the lead they dashed

forward. They had almost reached the brush when Jenkins caught Ned by the arm and halted him.

'Saw somethin' skitter past that thar thicket,' he said in a low tone, nodding toward the spot, 'Might've been one o' them hombres.'

'Reckon we'd better circle 'em,' Harris said shortly. 'Go thet way,' pointing to the right, 'I'll go this way. We kin ketch 'em between us.'

The ranger dashed away as Ned had directed. The latter swung off toward the left and slipped into the brush. He heard a twig snap and flattened out instantly against a tree, saw a shadow rise suddenly a few feet ahead of him. He crouched and waited for a better view, his Colts ready in his hands. Minutes passed but nothing moved. He stepped out from behind the tree, threw himself sideways when he saw the shadow again and fired. The shadow swayed and crashed in the thick brush. He halted and waited, wanted to make certain that it wasn't a trick, then satisfied that he had gotten his man, he went forward again. He spied a tall figure some distance beyond, halted and studied it for a moment. It was Smith Jenkins. He started after the ranger, tripped over a rock and sprawled on all fours. He cursed softly, climbed to his feet and plunged ahead. The ranger heard him, turned and waited for him to draw near. Jenkins dragged him down behind a tree.

'Spot th' other feller?' Harris asked in a whisper.

'Shore did,' Jenkins answered in a low tone. 'Keep outta this. This feller belongs t'me.'

He slipped away. Ned crouched, watched him advance. A rifle cracked close by, then a Colt roared twice in answer. Ned arose and peered into the darkness ahead. He saw a bulky figure stagger out from behind a tree, lean against another tree for a moment, then the figure tottered away and toppled over. A minute later Smith Jenkins came striding back.

'Reckon that's that,' he said briefly.

Together they trudged out through the brush toward where they had left their horses.

'That's two less we'll have t' worry 'bout,' the ranger said. 'Got yourn furst shot, eh?'

Harris nodded briefly.

'Had to,' he said simply. 'It was him or me an' I didn't aim t' hev it be me.'

They mounted shortly and rode forward again through the brush and through the tall trees beyond them. Jenkins reloaded his gun as they went on. It was probably after they had covered a mile that a horse neighed, startlingly near. They halted at once and looked about quickly. There was no one in sight, nothing but the horse they had stumbled over. He came forward out of the shadows and followed them into the thicket where the men dismounted and tethered their horses.

'Reckon thar must be a house up ahead,' Harris said in an undertone.

'Aim t' surround it?' the ranger asked.

'Wa-al,' Ned answered, 'We'll have a look at it furst, then we'll figger out th' next move.'

They sauntered forward again presently, treading as lightly as they could. It was slow going due to the darkness, hidden rocks and the thick brush. Presently Harris nudged Jenkins and halted.

'That's the house,' Ned said. 'See it, yonder behin' th' trees?' He pointed in its direction.

Jenkins looked quickly.

'Uh-huh,' he answered. 'There's a light in one o' th' windows.' He strode forward.

'Hol' on a minute,' Harris called softly.

The ranger retraced his steps.

'I'm gonna drift aroun' toward th' back o' th' house,' Ned said shortly. 'you cover th' front.'

'Yuh bet.'

'Jest one more thing,' Harris added. 'Case I see th' girl an' git a chance t' bust in, I'll letcha know. Then yuh drift away and squat down

154

behin' one of them trees facin' th' house and start blastin' away.'

'Go on.'

'They'll prob'bly shoot back at yuh, see? Thet'll gimme a chance t' git inside, git th' girl and git out agin,' he concluded.

'Right,' Jenkins answered. 'On'y if you don't git out in a hurry, I'll come after yuh.'

'I'm runnin' this,' Harris said curtly. 'Do like I said. Keep blastin' away at th' front o' th' house an' stay put. Understan'?'

'Yep. Go 'head.'

Ned slipped away through the brush and skirted the house. When he reached a spot opposite the rear, he swung away from the brush and approached the house. When he was within reach of the house he dropped down and crawled forward on hands and knees. He halted presently and looked up. A door was close at hand. With the greatest care he tried the knob. It turned easily; the door swung back on noiseless hinges.

He paused for a moment, peering inside, listening intently. Inside was a dim light. He could hear voices. He stepped inside, softly closing the door behind him. For another moment he stood still, waiting for his eyes to grow accustomed to the faint light. He looked about carefully. He was in what appeared to be a kitchen. Across the room was a partially closed door through which streamed a thin shaft of light. He glided silently across the room and peered through the door crack. At a table in the middle of the room sat three men. Two of them Ned recognized at once. One was Hawkins. The second was the man who had nudged Hawkins on the trail, evidently to let him know that the kidnapping had succeeded. The third man was big and burly and on his shirt front hung a silver star. Ned gasped. It was the sheriff of Deadwood.

He drew away suddenly when he heard a sound behind him. He turned quickly. There was something in the corner of the room, something that breathed with an effort. He glided into the darkness and stared hard. It was Carol Hall, bound and gagged. He bent over her swiftly.

'It's me,' he whispered, 'Harris.'

She made a gurgling sound in answer. Swiftly he untied the gag, then he freed her ankles and wrists. He gripped her slim shoulders with his big hands.

'Yuh awright?' he asked in a low tone.

'Yes,' she answered. 'I knew you'd come for me.'

He helped her to her feet, led her to the door.

'Step outside,' he whispered, 'An' wait thar. Not in front o' th' door. Better leave thet clear case I hev t' git out in a hurry.'

He opened the door noiselessly, helped her out, then he closed it again. Silently he glided across the room to the connecting, partially closed door. He was curious to know what Hawkins and the sheriff were talking about. He tripped over a rope, the one with which Carol had been bound, glared at it and kicked it out of his way. His boot toe banged violently against a chair and it crashed against the wall and slid along the floor and toppled over.

There was a sudden outcry from the other room. Chairs were hurled aside as men sprang to their feet. Ned leaped for the back door, fell over the chair and sprawled on his face. A gun roared and a bullet splintered the connecting door and showered him with splinters. He cursed, fought his way to his knees, whipped out one of his Colts and blazed away with abandon. In the other room something crashed, plunging the room into complete darkness. He chuckled inwardly. He hadn't seen anything of a lamp when he had looked in there before, but one of his stray shots had found it and smashed it. He got to his feet, tore open the back door and lurched out.

'Come on,' he yelled.

He spied Carol crouching just beyond the door, against the building, raced over and swung her up into his arms. A roar of pistol

157

shots blasted the front of the house. It was Smith Jenkins, slightly tardy, swinging into action. Those inside the darkened house returned his fire. He raced over the ground toward the brush. He heard the clatter of horses' hoofs, looked up quickly and saw two mounted men sweeping down upon them. A bullet skidded past Ned's feet. He dove headlong into the brush. Carol slid out of his arms and rolled away, safely out of range. Ned twisted around, whipped out his Colts and blazed away. He heard a horse scream, saw it rear up on its hind legs and crash over backwards, pinning its rider beneath it. The second horseman slid to a halt. He swung out of the saddle, his guns belching flame. A bullet tore Ned's hat from his head, a second grazed his cheek. Now his Colts roared angrily, protestingly. The man staggered, dropped his guns, fell against his horse and crumpled to the ground.

'Reckon thet takes keer o' them kidnappers,' he said half-aloud.

Another figure raced along the side of the house. It was the figure of a tall man. Ned raised his Colts, studied the approaching figure for a moment, saw that it was Smith Jenkins. He holstered his guns and stepped out of the brush.

'Over hyar,' he called.

158

Jenkins panted to a halt beside him.

'Got 'er?' he asked breathlessly.

'Yep,' Harris answered briefly.

He stepped into the brush again, reappeared in a minute with Carol in his arms.

'I brought th' horses up yonder a piece,' the ranger said quickly. 'Foller me.'

He wheeled and raced away, Ned pounding along at his heels. Minutes later they swung away from the house and halted in a thicket screened by tall trees. It was a moment's work to mount. With Carol on the saddle in front of him, Ned wheeled the big black and sent him plunging away through the brush. The roan drew alongside.

They heard the front door of the house bang against the side of the building. They heard a cry, heard two shots sing past them. The roan jerked to a halt. Jenkins wheeled without a word and cantered back. Ned pulled the big black back on his haunches, wheeled and watched the ranger ride toward the house. He saw a tall figure of a man come down the path from the house, saw fire flame from his hand. Jenkins fired twice in answer. The shots echoed through the countryside. The man took a step forward along the path, rose up on his toes for a moment and pitched forward on his face. Jenkins wheeled his mount and galloped back. He pulled alongside of Harris.

159

'Reckon Hawkins is gonna need a hull new gang,' he said.

Together they went on again. Presently the rhythmic clatter of pounding hoofs died away.

CHAPTER TWELVE

On through the forest they rode, swept through the heavy brush that abounded, thundered past the tall, stout, stolid trees that dotted the land. Shadows leaped up about them, darted at them like far-reaching monsters' hands, whisked fleetingly over them and faded away before them into the enveloping darkness of the night. Carol breathed a sigh of relief when they left the last of the wooded section behind them and burst through the barrier of brush and into the open. They drew rein when they reached the bank of the river. Smith Jenkins edged his mount alongside Harris'.

'Which way?' he asked.

Harris shrugged his shoulder.

'Reckon it don't make much diff'rence so long's we keep goin',' he answered shortly. 'Might be a good idea t' put distance between us an' them fellers back thar, y'know.'

'Fellers? What fellers?' the ranger

demanded. 'Anybody left b'side Hawkins?'

Ned nodded grimly, thoughtfully.

'Jest one feller,' he said in answer. 'Th' sheriff o' Deadwood.'

'Th' sheriff?' Jenkins echoed. 'What 'bout 'im? What's he got t' do wit' Hawkins?'

Harris grinned fleetingly.

'I didn't stop t' ask,' he answered. 'Course I got kinda curious when I seen him thar, settin' an' palaverin' nice an' friendly-like with thet Hawkins. I sidled up t' th' door t' listen but in th' dark m' feet got tangled up wit' some rope an' a chair an' furst thing I knowed, I was sprawled out all over th' place. Me hittin' th' floor like a herd o' stampedin' steers is whut started th' ruction.'

The ranger was silent for a moment.

'Funny 'bout that sheriff,' he mused. 'Powwowin' wit' a skunk like Hawkins. I been hearin' some tall yarns 'bout things in Deadwood an' this kinda ties in wit' 'em.' He frowned in thought. 'Now what d'yuh s'pose a lawman'd be talkin' 'bout to a feller like Hawkins?'

'Dunno.'

'Wish I knew,' Jenkins said. 'Looks t' me like there's dirty-work afoot.'

'Meanin'?'

'That Hawkins an' th' sheriff are in cahoots 'bout somethin',' Jenkins said without

161

hesitation.

Carol turned in the saddle.

'Would it interest either of you to know that a roll of bills was passed across the table?' she asked.

'Go on,' the ranger commanded.

'The door was open then and I could see both hands and money on the table. Someone arose, dragged me across the room and left me in the corner of the room. Then the door was slammed shut. It unlatched itself a little later, but I was too far away to see anything else,' she concluded.

'H'm,' was all the comment that Jenkins volunteered. 'That ties up th' sheriff wit' Hawkins but it don't prove anythin' else.'

'Not th' way I see it,' Harris shot back. 'Th' passin' o' money means one o' two things, mebbe both. Somebody coulda been payin' fer somethin' done or somebody was buyin' somethin'. Yuh kin bet all the booze in Deadwood thet it wasn't Hawkins passin' th' money. He musta been on th' receivin' end wit' th' sheriff doin' th' passin'.'

'I'm still listenin',' Jenkins said. 'An' still waitin' t' be convinced.'

Harris turned quickly to Carol.

'Thet map. You still got it?' he asked.

She shook her head slowly.

'No,' she answered quietly. 'They found it

162

hidden in the sole of my boot.'

Jenkins groaned.

'H'm,' Ned said. 'Thar's yo' answer, Mister. Thet's what th' sheriff was payin' fer.'

'But, doggone it, Ma'm,' Jenkins said. 'How come yuh didn't say somethin' 'bout it before we left.'

'Keep yo' shirt on, Ranger,' Harris said curtly. 'Mebbe she didn't hev much uva chance t' say anythin' in all thet gun throwin'.'

'Yeah,' Jenkins admitted begrudgingly. 'Reckon that's right.' He leaned over. 'Don't worry none, Ma'm,' he said reassuringly. 'We'll git it back.'

Harris grinned.

'Shore, but how?'

'Heck,' Jenkins answered. 'We'll find a way.'

Carol laughed lightly.

'Well, now that that's settled,' she said, 'do you think you could concentrate for a moment on the subject of food?'

'Ain't no trouble a-tall, concentratin' on it,' Jenkins answered with a sly grin. 'It's gettin' th' food that worries me. How 'bout it, Harris?'

'Left my stuff back in th' hills when I lit out after Hawkins,' Ned said. 'Prob'bly all et by now wit' all them wolves roamin' aroun'.'

'Well, there's no sense thinking about it,'

163

Carol said presently. 'Don't you think we ought to go on or something?'

'Might's well,' Harris replied. 'Don't s'pose any chuck wagons'll come this way. Come on. We'll go 'cross th' way we come.'

Carol looked sharply at the water. She turned quickly to Harris.

'Br-r-r,' she said. 'It looks cold.'

Jenkins laughed.

'Shore does but that ain't nuthin' t' th' way it feels,' he said. 'I know 'cause I was in it.'

The big black moved off. At the water's edge he halted, raised his head and whinnied. The roan came up alongside of him, looked at him curiously for a moment.

'G'wan,' Harris said briefly.

The big black stepped into the water hesitantly. The roan, spurred by Jenkins, bounded ahead, plunged into the water, snorted loudly and shot a spray of water into the air. Now the big black was in the water; presently it swirled up around him, then he went on undaunted. Carol clung to Ned; watched the swift-current fearfully. Then they were past mid-stream and her fears abated. Minutes later the horses trod on land, panted up the bank, halted and shook themselves. Then they moved on again. Their iron shoes rang out sharply as they clattered over the rocky terrain. They swung southward again toward the shadowy hills. Now there was no brush to ride through, and soon too there were no tall, broad-trunked trees to skirt. There was instead the cold, hard ground and sun-bleached boulders, strangely white and moon-lit.

In the distance they heard a snarl, a yelp of pain, then more snarls. Carol turned quickly.

'Wolves?' she asked anxiously.

'Uh-huh,' Harris answered.

Nervously she watched each boulder, tensed each time she saw a shadow on the trail ahead. Each time that they passed unmolested, she relaxed, but only for the moment, breathed a sigh of relief only to stiffen expectantly and go through the identical procedure when the next boulder loomed up. Suddenly the snarling they had heard before broke out anew, but this time it was startlingly close. Two gray-back wolves bounded across the trail. The horses reared up in panic and backed away. One of the wolves, apparently the pursuer, leaped upon his mate and bore him to the ground. They rolled over, snarled and tore at each other with flashing teeth, oblivious to the fact that three humans sat on their horses not more than ten feet away and watched as they fought to the death. The attacking wolf swarmed over his mate, sought and got a death-grip on the latter's throat and hung on grimly despite the efforts of the second wolf to fight his way free. Jenkins edged the roan closer. His Colt flashed in his hand. His gun roared, flamed a second time. The attacking wolf sank to the ground. The second wolf leaped upon him, tore at him furiously, ripping his throat with flashing, blood-stained teeth. Carol turned her head quickly. The Colt belched fire. The surviving wolf went down in a heap, dragging himself beyond the trail when the gun flamed again. This time the wolf slumped and lay still. Jenkins edged closer, holstered his smoking gun, and beckoned to them to follow.

The roan trotted past the motionless figures. The big black snorted and swung wide of them. On they went then into the hills with nothing to break the stillness of the silent night but the rhythmic beat of iron-shod hoofs. Carol relaxed and bowed her head. Jenkins checked his mount, ranged alongside of Harris'.

'Thought o' somethin'?' he asked shortly.

'Nope,' Harris answered. 'Been thinkin' about grub an' wishin' we had some. Looks like she's plumb wore out. She ain't had nothin' in a hull day.'

'Me neither.'

'Shucks,' Ned answered, 'You ain't a girl.'

They rode together then, far into the night.

Once or twice the big black raised his head, but each time he went on again. Jenkins looked at him sharply.

'What ails 'im?' he asked finally.

'Dunno,' Harris answered. 'Maybe he smells somethin' thet we don't.'

Jenkins grinned.

'Smells somethin', eh? Hope he smells somethin' thet's good t'eat,' he said. He glanced over at Carol. Now she lay back against Ned. 'Sleepin'?'

'Reckon so,' came Harris' answer.

'Po're kid,' the ranger said. 'She's shore had plenty o' excitement these last couple o' days.'

The big black halted. Jenkins looked up again.

'What now?' he asked shortly.

Harris sniffed the air.

'Don' tell me yuh smell somethin' too,' the ranger said. He stood up in his stirrups and sniffed loudly. 'Don't smell a thing.'

'Doggone it,' Harris said admiringly. 'Thet big feller kin smell grub a mile 'way.'

'You're plumb loco.'

'Yeah? Ef thet ain't bacon I'm smellin',' Ned said, 'yuh kin hog-tie me an' throw me t' th' wolves.'

Jenkins snorted scornfully.

'Yuh been wishin' so hard that you're smellin' what you'd like t' be eatin',' he said

167

presently. He stood up again in his stirrups and sniffed. He turned quickly, excitedly. 'Doggone it,' he cried. 'Blamed if I ain't smellin' somethin', too.'

'Then mebbe I ain't so loco?'

'If y'are, Harris,' the ranger answered, 'then I am, too.'

He gripped the reins with renewed vigor.

'Come on,' he said.

'Hol' on,' Harris said quickly. 'Don't go bustin' off like that. Git offen yo' horse and hev a look 'round furst. Mebbe thet feller thet's doin' the cooking ain't th' sociable kind.'

Jenkins laughed lightly.

'So long's he's got bacon,' he replied. 'He don't hafta be sociable.'

He slid out of the saddle and went forward on foot. Presently he disappeared from view. Harris glanced skyward. It was getting light now. He turned and looked at the snow-capped peaks to the rear. Now they were shedding their shadowy appearance and taking on definite form. The hills too cast off their blackness and the faint light from the awakening sky gave them a grim outline that grew more distinct and pronounced with each minute. Jenkins came scurrying back.

'It's bacon shore 'nuff,' he reported. 'An' a hull pan full. There ain't jest one feller, but

two, an' they're jest 'bout th' meanest lookin'
critters I ever seen.'

Harris nodded.

'Uh-huh,' he said briefly.

He touched Carol's shoulder lightly. Her
bowed head came up slowly.

'Carol,' he said.

She stirred, sighed and opened her eyes.

'Thet grub yuh was concentratin' on
before,' Harris said presently, 'yuh still got a
hankerin' fer it?'

'Grub?' she repeated.

Harris nodded.

'Y'know, food.'

'Oh, yes,' she answered quickly. She
grimaced and rubbed one sleeping arm. 'I'm
famished.'

Harris swung out of the saddle. He turned
and held out his arms.

'Come on,' he said.

She swung one leg over the saddle horn,
kicked her other foot out of the stirrup and
slid down. He caught her and set her down on
the ground lightly.

'Th' fellers doin' th' cookin' fer us,' he said
shortly, 'ain't th' sociable kind. Jenkins an'
me'll jest amble over an' see 'bout gittin' 'em
to act friendly-like. Yuh stay hyar wit' th'
horses 'till we git back.'

She looked up at him quickly.

169

'Do you think they'll refuse?' she asked.

He laughed lightly.

She laughed, too.

'Heck, no,' he answered. 'Ain't I got th' law wit' me?' He turned to Jenkins. 'Come on, ranger.'

Harris turned and strode away. Jenkins followed at his heels. They swung down the trail and disappeared behind one of the ever-present boulders. They went on a ways then Jenkins caught Harris' arm and pointed.

'They're down there,' he said, in a low tone.

'Uh-huh.'

'Mebbe we oughtn't t' bust right in,' Jenkins said.

'Don't aim t',' Ned answered. 'We'll hev a look furst, then we kin figger out our greetin'.'

They went forward again, noiselessly. There were boulders and rocks ahead and they shifted from one to the other to avoid detection. Jenkins nudged Harris.

'Git behin' that rock,' he said in an undertone, nodding toward a huge rock some few feet away. 'An' have a look.'

Harris slipped past him and reached the spot Jenkins had pointed out, and looked down into a small, rock-encircled clearing. In the middle of the clearing was a small fire. A burly man was squatting beside it, handling a

170

pan of sizzling bacon. Another man knelt a few feet away. He was settling a pot of steaming coffee on a square, flat rock. Ned studied the men carefully for a moment. Both were burly and in the light they looked just as mean and 'ornery' as Jenkins had described them. Both, Harris noted, wore heavy Colts against their thighs. He turned and beckoned to Jenkins who crept to his side.

'Ornery lookin' like you said,' Ned whispered.

Jenkins nodded.

'What d'yuh aim t' do?' he asked.

'I'm jest gonna stan' up an' walk right in,' Harris answered in a low tone. 'Yuh stay hyar an' kinda cover me. Whut we do af'er thet depends on whut happens.'

'Right,' Jenkins answered.

He whipped out his gun.

'Go 'head,' he said. 'I'll be ready t' blast if them fellers draw on yuh.'

Harris nodded, got to his feet and sauntered forward into the clearing. He halted presently.

'Howdy, gents,' he said.

The pan of sizzling bacon halted in mid-air with such abruptness that some of the hot fat spewed out over the hand of the man handling it. He cursed loudly, turned and looked over at Harris, got to his feet and licked his burned fingers with his tongue. The second man had just put down the coffee pot. He wheeled like a flash, whipped out his gun, leveled it and got to his feet. The man stopped licking his fingers for a moment and sauntered forward a bit.

'Yuh hadn't ought come sneakin' up on a feller thetaway,' he said angrily. 'I'm burned half t' death, dang blast yore hide!'

Harris grinned lightly.

'Knew a feller once thet uster put dirt on a burn,' he said.

'Did it do 'im any good?'

Harris shook his head.

'Nope. Last time I heered 'bout 'im, somebody told me he set fire t' 'nother feller's barn an' couldn't dig his way out from under,' he concluded.

The man gave him an icy stare, turned and sauntered back to the fire. His companion looked Harris over carefully.

'Whut yuh doin' hyar, stranger?' he asked.

Harris grinned fleetingly.

'Jest passin',' he answered. 'Didn't know thet bacon could smell so temptin'.'

'Whar's yo' hoss?' the man asked.

'Back thar a piece,' Ned answered, turning his head slightly and nodding in the direction of the trail. 'M' pardner's waitin' wit' 'im.'

'Yo' pardner, eh?' the man repeated. 'Go git 'em.'

'Thet's mighty generous o' yuh,' Harris said. 'Shore yuh got 'nuff fer all o' us?'

'Yuh ain't gonna git much,' the burly man replied curtly. 'This ain't no chuck wagon, y'know.'

Ned laughed, turned and strode away. Hardly had he gone than the man with the burned fingers stepped to his companion's side and whispered to him. The burly man nodded, shoved his gun into his holster, nodded again and laughed. Harris strode past the rock behind which Jenkins was crouched.

'Come on,' Harris said in a low tone without halting.

Jenkins followed him, keeping low to avoid being seen by the men in the clearing. A few feet away, Ned halted.

'Well?' the ranger demanded.

'Yuh heard whut was said,' Ned said. 'Didn't yuh?'

'Shore did.'

'Whut d'yuh make o' them critters?' Harris asked.

The ranger shrugged his shoulder.

'Dunno. How 'bout you?'

Harris frowned fleetingly.

'Wa-al, I ain't 'zactly positive 'bout it,' he said slowly. 'But I got a'idea thet them fellers an' me hev met before.'

'Oh, yeah?'

173

Harris nodded briefly.

'Uh-huh,' he went on. 'An' ef I ain't plumb cock-eyed, them fellers are deputies.'

The ranger whistled softly.

'Think they reco'nized yuh?' he asked shortly.

Harris grinned.

'Shucks, no,' he answered. 'None o' them fellers ever got close 'nuff t' git a good look at me.' He paused for a moment. 'Now I wonder ...' his voice trailed away.

Jenkins eyed him questioningly.

'Yuh wonder what?'

'Nuthin',' Harris answered. 'I'd shore like fer th' girl t' hev a look at them fellers.'

'That's easy,' Jenkins said.

'Go git 'er, willya?' Ned asked. 'I'll sorta hang aroun' an' see whut them fellers are doin'.'

'Right.'

The ranger stepped past him, slipped away and dashed back to where they had left Carol and the horses. Ned dropped down, made his way forward toward the huge rock and peered out cautiously. One of the men, the burly one, was examining his gun. His companion, the one who had burned his fingers was pouring himself a cup of coffee. Once or twice he glanced at his hand and cursed softly. Harris turned quickly when he heard a light step

174

behind him. It was Carol Hall. He reached up, caught her hand and drew her down beside the rock. He caught a fleeting glimpse of Jenkins as he slid to a halt behind another huge rock.

'Look at them fellers,' Ned commanded in a whisper.

Carol leaned out a bit, then she withdrew hurriedly. Her eyes were gleaming.

'Ned,' she whispered excitedly.

'Yeah?'

'Those men,' she whispered quickly. 'I've seen them before.'

'Uh-huh. Whar?'

'They came to that house with the man who passed the money across the table,' she said in a low tone. 'They had silver stars on their shirts.'

'Thet's all I wanna know,' he answered grimly. 'Hustle back t' th' horses an' stay thar. Ef yuh hear shots, don't git excited. Understan'?'

She nodded quickly.

'You'll be careful, won't you?' she asked.

'Shore,' he replied.

She turned and slipped away as noiselessly as she had come. Harris turned and beckoned to Jenkins to join him. The ranger made his way forward.

'Well?' he asked.

'Carol reco'nized them fellers,' Ned answered. 'They come t' th' house wit' th' sheriff.'

'Uh-huh. Anythin' else?'

'Wa-al,' Ned mused, 'I'm wonderin' ef they ain't carryin' that blamed map t' town fer th' sheriff.'

Jenkins gasped.

'Doggone it, Harris,' he said quickly. 'I'll bet a-plenty they are.' He eyed Ned admiringly. 'I gotta hand it t' yuh.'

Harris grinned lightly.

'Mebbe yuh'd better wait an' see ef I'm right b'fore yuh start handin' out bouquets,' he answered.

'I'll take a chance on that,' the ranger maintained stoutly. 'What are you aimin' to do?'

'I'm goin' back thar,' Ned said quietly. 'Alone.'

'Huh?'

'Yuh heerd me. I'm gonna tell 'em yuh ain't hungry,' Harris went on. 'Ef they do whut I figger they'll do, you an' yo' six-gun'll come in handy.'

'Yuh mean that I'm t' stay hyar? Behin' this rock again?' Jenkins demanded.

Harris nodded. Jenkins frowned, gave him a sidelong glance. Finally he shrugged his shoulder.

'Well, if that's the way yuh want it,' he said with a trace of resignation in his voice, 'that's the way it's gonna be. Go 'head.'

Ned stepped back from behind the rock and strode into the clearing. The burly man looked up and sauntered forward, his thumbs hooked in his sagging gun belt.

'Whut took yuh s'long, stranger?' he asked. 'An' whar's yo' pardner?'

'Said he ain't hungry,' Ned answered briefly.

The burly man arched his heavy eyebrows.

'Thet so? Wa-al, go 'head an' help y'self,' he said with forced casualness.

'Thanks.'

Harris strolled toward the fire. The man with the burned fingers looked up, nodded and straightened up. At a quick nod from his companion he turned away. The burly man stepped forward, whipped out his gun and jammed it into Harris' ribs.

'Reach,' he said coldly.

Ned's hands went up slowly.

'Charley,' the burly man said shortly. 'Go git th' other feller.'

The man named Charley laughed lightly.

'Shore, Bill,' he answered briefly.

He hitched up his pants and trudged away. When he came abreast of the rock something caused him to look up. He halted, stared hard and gulped. Directly in front of him stood a tall youth and in the tall youth's hand was a levelled Colt. There was something very definite of purpose and very business-like in the tall youth's manner. Charley made no attempt to draw his gun.

'Elevate 'em,' he heard the tall youth say curtly.

Charley swallowed hard. Surprises always affected his nervous system. Slowly but surely his hands climbed over his head. Bill happened to glance over. He frowned at what he saw. For a brief moment he forgot about Harris, turned halfway as if he contemplated snapping a shot at Charley's captor. That brief moment of uncertainty proved Bill's undoing. An iron thunderbolt swished and collided with his unprotected jaw. His gun flew out of his hand. He went down on all fours and stared hard when he found himself face to face with the hard ground. He shook his muddled head and when he looked again, the ground was still there, not more than six inches from his face. He managed to get to his knees, in fact he had almost straightened up when lightning struck. Bill went over backwards like a felled tree, quivered for a moment and finally lay still.

Swiftly Harris bent over him. He rummaged through Bill's spacious pockets.

Presently he straightened up.

'Hey,' he yelled.

'Yeah?'

'I got it,' he yelled again, triumphantly, waving aloft a folded sheet of heavy paper.

CHAPTER THIRTEEN

Charley was a very subdued and considerably crestfallen man when Smith Jenkins, nudging him on with the muzzle of his gun, drove him back into the clearing. He had heard strange, crunching sounds behind him, but Jenkins' gun, jammed hard against his belly, had speedily and forthwith removed all desire to turn and investigate the sounds. He saw Harris standing just beyond the fire rubbing the knuckles of his right hand against the palm of his left hand. He turned his head slightly and stared with widening eyes at Bill who lay flat on his broad back some few feet away. Bill was strangely motionless. There was a curious, crimson, deepening welt on one cheek as if someone had held a branding iron against it. Then too, there were a few flecks of blood on his chin and from a corner of his twisted mouth a tiny crimson rivulet surged downward over his sagging chin and came to

179

rest upon his dark, rough shirt. While Charley was staring at his fallen companion, Jenkins nodded to Harris who stepped forward, yanked out Charley's gun and handed it to the ranger.

Jenkins looked down at the sprawled figure. He shook his head, turned and caught Harris' eye.

'That feller's gonna have a big head fer a week,' he said presently. 'Betcha he's havin' nightmares right now.'

Harris grinned lightly.

'Ef his haid's any harder'n his jaw,' he answered, 'I'm shore glad I didn't hafta hit it.'

'What yuh aimin' t' do wit' 'im?' the ranger asked.

'Reckon we'll jest tie 'im up so's he don't git ideas,' Ned said. 'After we've sorta et a little, we'll figger out th' rest. Git a rope, willya?'

Jenkins nodded.

'How 'bout this feller?' he asked, nodding toward Charley.

Harris grinned again.

'Shucks,' he answered. 'He looks right peaceable t' me. Don't think he aims t' start nuthin'.'

Charley looked up quickly.

'Heck, no,' he said quickly, looking from one to the other. 'I'm so doggoned peaceable, I kin feel wings sproutin'.'

Both Harris and Jenkins laughed.

'Set down,' the former said briefly.

Charley needed no urging. He sat down in a hurry, cross-legged, and looked up again.

'An' don't git no fool ideas,' Ned said shortly. ''Less yuh aims t' hev them wings really sprout.'

Smith Jenkins hurried away.

'Jenkins,' Harris called.

The ranger halted and looked back.

'Bring th' girl an' th' horses, willya?' Ned asked. 'This bacon's been fryin' so long, it's prob'bly tougher'n thet feller's jaw. Reckon th' coffee's still good, though, so shake a leg.'

Jenkins nodded and strode out of sight. Harris turned his attention to Charley. The latter squirmed uncomfortably under Ned's appraising gaze.

'Whut's yo' name?' Harris asked presently.

'Who, me?'

Harris frowned.

'Willis, Charley Willis.'

'An' him?' Ned asked, nodding toward the outstretched figure beyond them.

'Bill Severs.'

Harris was silent for a minute.

'Deputies, ain'tcha?' he asked presently.

Charley nodded without thinking, then he looked up at Harris questioningly, his eyes wide with surprise. 'How'd yuh know thet,

181

Mister?' he asked with obvious wonder.

'Ne'er mind,' Harris answered. 'Whar yuh fellers headed fer?'

'Town,' Charley answered briefly. 'Deadwood City.'

'Uh-huh.' Harris produced the paper he had taken from Bill's pocket. He held it up for Charley to see. 'An' whar was yuh takin' this?'

Charley looked at it for a moment, opened his mouth to speak, evidently thought better of it and closed his mouth.

'Yuh seen it b'fore, ain'tcha?' Ned asked.

Charley hesitated again.

'Talk,' Harris said curtly. His hand slid down and came to a halt upon the butts of his Colts.

Charley's eyes swept down from Ned's face to the heavy guns that sagged his belt. He swallowed hard and looked up again, slowly. The color seemed to have drained out of his face.

'It's a map, ain't it?' he asked, falteringly.

Harris made no answer. He looked coldly at Charley and waited for him to continue. Charley turned fleetingly toward the prone Bill Severs as if he were pleading with him to rise and help him. There was no answering movement from Bill, nothing save a momentary twitching of one leg. Charley turned slowly, helplessly, to face his captor.

182

'I'll tell yuh, Mister,' he said finally. 'Th' sheriff gev' it t' Bill.'

He breathed a deep sigh of relief and sat back, but in a flash Harris was upon him. He gripped Charley's shirt front and jerked him to his feet.

'Talk, yuh yaller bellied skunk,' Ned said through his teeth, 'Or I'll tear it outta yuh.'

Charley's face was a sickly white.

'Shore, Mister,' he managed to say. 'I was aimin' t' tell yuh. Th' sheriff gev it t' Bill an' tol' 'im t' take it t' town an' register th' claim in his name. In Bill's name, y'know. Thet's th' hull truth, s' help me.'

Harris threw Charley from him. The white-faced deputy landed on the seat of his pants some distance away. At that moment Jenkins appeared. Carol trudging along beside him. The horses followed at their heels. The ranger and the girl halted and looked first at the dazed Charley, then at Harris. There was a rope slung over Jenkins' shoulder. He strode forward, slipped the rope off his shoulder and held it out to Ned.

'Reckon you'd better take it,' the ranger said briefly. 'This bum arm o' mine ain't much uva help when it comes t' tyin' up things.'

Ned nodded, took the rope and strode over to the prostrate Severs. He bent over him,

183

looped a slipknot over Bill's right wrist, then over the man's left wrist. The knot was yanked tight and another knot looped over Bill's ankles. Presently, Harris looked up.

'Com'ere, Willis,' he called.

Charley got to his feet slowly. He shook his head sadly, trudged over as directed.

'Squat,' Ned said briefly.

Charley 'squatted' without a word. He put his hands behind him. The free end of the rope was promptly looped over his wrists, then it was jerked taut. Carol, standing beside the horses, as Jenkins had left her, watched quietly. Presently, Harris straightened up. He glanced at Severs, then at Charley Willis who sighed deeply, forlornly, with an air of helplessness and resignation. As Carol watched, she saw Charley look down at Severs and shake his head sadly. Slowly Ned turned away and trudged over to Carol's side. When he halted beside her, she looked up at him and smiled.

'From the look of things,' she said in a low tone, 'it's evident that those men weren't particularly sociable.'

He laughed softly.

'Wa-al,' he drawled in answer, 'th' feller takin' a nap was kinda stubborn an' ornery 'bout it in th' beginnin' an' needed a little persuadin'. Yuh kin see fer y'self thet he ain't

184

objectin' none now. As fer th' other feller,' he smiled fleetingly, 'soon's he seen th' error o' his ways, he was peaceable.'

She glanced at Willis, then she looked up at Harris again.

'So much so that you thought it best to tie him up anyway?' she asked, smilingly.

There was a twinkle in his eye. There was nothing hard about them now. They were blue-gray, soft, warm and full of depth.

'Figgered he wouldn't change his mind too sudden-like ef his hands was tied,' he answered gravely.

She turned and looked over toward the fire. Smith Jenkins was bending over it, watching the coffee pot he had discovered resting on a flat rock a few feet away. Harris followed her eyes, watched her for a moment, curiously, wonderingly.

'You were gone so long,' he heard her say presently in a quiet but almost reproachful tone. 'I was afraid that something had happened.' Slowly she turned to face him again. Her eyes searched his face, swept downward and came to an abrupt halt when they reached his right hand. 'Your hand,' she said quickly, looking up at him again, 'it's bleeding. Are you badly hurt?'

'Bleedin'?'

He brought the hand up, glanced at it and

185

pressed it gently against his shirt. When he drew it away there was a faint, crimson stain on the shirt. 'It's nuthin',' he said briefly. 'Musta skinned th' knuckles on thet feller,' he said, nodding toward Severs.

She turned too and looked at the prone figure of Bill Severs. She felt a strange glow within her, a warm feeling of pride. It was primitive, but womanlike, this pride in a man who had fought for her and triumphed. She looked up quickly when Smith Jenkins joined them.

'Reckon th' coffee's all right,' he announced. He looked questioningly at Harris. 'What yuh been doin' t' that feller?' he asked. 'Th' one yuh called Willis? He looks kinda white aroun' th' gills.'

Harris grinned.

'Nuthin' much,' he answered briefly.

'That's what I figgered,' the ranger said dryly. 'Yuh fin' out anythin' worth tellin'?'

'Some.'

'Well?' Jenkins asked, impatiently.

'Them two fellers were takin' th' map t' town,' Ned said.

The ranger's eyebrows went up.

'Oh, yeah? What fer?'

'Seems like th' sheriff give it t' them an' tol' 'em to register th' claim,' Harris continued. 'Leastways, in thet feller Severs' name.'

186

'Severs?'

'Th' feller takin' a nap,' Ned said with a nod in Severs' direction.

The ranger whistled softly.

'Doggone,' he said. A grin spread over his face. 'Yuh couldn't hev come no closer t' knowin' what they was up t' if you'da been settin' in on that powwow y'self. What yuh aimin' t' do next?'

Harris shrugged his shoulder.

'Dunno. Ain't figgered it out yet,' he replied shortly. He looked at Carol again. 'How's coffee sound t' yuh?'

She laughed lightly.

'Heavenly,' she answered. 'Just lead me to it.'

'C'mon,' Jenkins said.

Carol needed no urging. She turned without another word and followed the ranger toward the fire. Halfway, she turned and looked back and saw that Harris had made no attempt to follow them. Instead, he was standing just where they had left him, beside the horses. There was, she quickly noted, a frown on his face, a deepening frown, too.

'Smith,' she said.

The ranger turned to her, saw her looking back at Harris and halted.

'Somethin' wrong?' Jenkins called.

Harris looked up and shook his head.

187

'Nope,' he answered. 'Jest thinkin'.' He was silent again for a moment. 'Better git y'selves some o' that coffee.'

'What 'bout you?' the ranger asked.

Ned grinned.

'Doggone it,' he answered, 'cain't yuh let a feller 'lone when he's tryin' t' think?'

Jenkins snorted loudly.

'Huh,' he said clearly and scornfully. 'Yuh shore look like a sick calf when you're thinkin'.'

'Oh, yeah?' came Harris' retort. 'Reckon yuh ain't never done no thinkin' fer y'self an' mebbe yuh ain't never seen thet face o' yourn. Ef yuh ever git a look at it in a glass, don't look at it too sudden-like. Th' shock's liable t' kill yuh.'

Jenkins caught Carol's eye and grinned.

'Dunno what we'd a' done if he wasn't 'long to do th' thinkin' for us,' he said presently. 'Looks like all we're good fer is t' drink coffee. Doggone it, we'll drink it, all right, every last drop o' it, too. Then we'll see if he kin think up some coffee fer 'imself when there ain't none left.'

She laughed, turned when he did and went on with him again toward the fire. They halted beside it. There were two battered and dented tin cups lying on the ground close by. Jenkins glanced at them, spied a canteen close

188

by, too, uncorked it and rinsed out the cups, tossed the canteen aside and handed Carol one of the cups. He bent over, touched the handle of the coffee pot and jerked his hand away hurriedly.

'Damn,' she heard him say.

He put his fingers to his lips and blew on them. He looked up, found her watching him, a look of amusement on her face. He managed a weak grin.

'Nearly burned 'em off,' he said sheepishly.

He dug inside his shirt and presently produced a heavy glove. He slipped it over his hand. Gingerly he touched the pot handle, smiled, tightened his grip on it, looked up at her and winked.

'There,' he said, obviously pleased with himself. 'Reckon that'll do th' trick. Betcha he couldn'ta done no better.'

He filled her cup, filled the other one for himself and straightened up. He raised his cup to his lips, sipped his coffee slowly, paused when he glanced at her and noticed that she hadn't even raised her own cup and lowered his when he saw that she was looking at Harris. He eyed her curiously for a moment, wondered what she was thinking about. She turned presently when she felt his eyes upon her and looked up at him.

'Smith,' he heard her say.

'Yeah?'

'Smith,' she said again. 'What's going to become of him?'

He glanced fleetingly at the tall figure standing beside the horses.

'Him? Y' mean Harris?'

She nodded slowly.

'Yes,' she said simply.

He shrugged his shoulder.

'Dunno,' he answered shortly. A frown deepened over his face. He lowered his cup and stared down at it for a moment. 'Been thinkin' 'bout that a hull lot.'

'So have I,' she said quietly.

He was silent for a minute, frowning again in thought.

''Course,' he began presently, 'there ain't no two ways 'bout it. I'm a lawman and th' law wants 'im. Still, I been hopin' that somethin' might happen, so's I wouldn'ta hafta do what I know I'm gonna do.' He shook his head for a moment. 'Shore wish it was somebody else 'stead o' him.'

He looked up again and studied the tall figure beyond them.

'There's somethin' 'bout him,' he said shortly, 'that ain't hard to like.'

She nodded in agreement.

'There's a lot o' fellers like him,' he continued. 'Allus make me think uva bunch o'

190

wild horses, mustangs, roamin' th' open prairie an' defyin' anyone t' ketch 'em an' tame 'em. Ever seen 'em? They're fine lookin', fast as lightnin', snortin' an' prancin' an' allus ready t' fight. Git up close t' them an' it's surprisin' t' fin' how gentle they kin be. Reckon he ain't no different from them.'

She nodded again.

'There is something about him, Smith,' she said slowly. 'It's something likeable, too, something hard to define, hard to point to and say "there it is." It's when you're really close to him that you become aware of it, when you seem to see him as he really is. It's something that takes hold of you, seems to tighten it's hold the longer you're near him and finally begins to grow on you.'

He studied her face as she spoke; nodded when she finished.

'He's so completely different from anyone I've ever known,' she continued. 'I wonder, Smith, if anyone ever really knew him or tried to understand him?'

'I wouldn't know much 'bout that,' he answered. 'But I shore do know a-plenty 'bout somethin' else.'

She looked at him quickly, questioningly.

'Yes?'

His face was set and grim.

'He ain't th' kind that jest gives in without

191

puttin' up a fight,' he said slowly. 'When th' time comes, it'll be him or me.' He raised his cup to his lips. 'Drink yo' coffee. He's a-comin'.'

CHAPTER FOURTEEN

Ned Harris came striding over to join them. Forewarned of his approach, Carol lowered her eyes and pretended not to see him; instead she appeared to be studying the contents of her cup. Ned halted in front of them and looked down at the coffee pot resting at Jenkins' feet.

'Finish all th' coffee?' he asked.

Carol looked up then.

'Oh, hello,' she said brightly.

Jenkins lowered his cup.

'Don't tell me yuh finished all yo' thinkin' s' soon?' he asked, mockingly.

Harris grinned lightly.

'How 'bout some coffee?' he asked.

'Well, how 'bout it?' the ranger asked. 'There's the pot. Help y'self. Don't 'spect me t'hand it t' yuh. G'wan, burn yo' own han's. I darn near burned mine off.'

'How 'bout a cup or somethin'?' Ned asked.

'Ain't got but two cups an' we're usin' 'em,'

192

Jenkins said. 'If yuh kin wait 'til I git finished, yuh kin hev mine.'

'Doggone yuh,' Harris retorted. 'Yuh been hangin' onter thet cup s' long, it's darn near growed onter yo' hand. Git done wit' it an' lemme hev it.'

Jenkins eyed him calmly.

'S'pose yuh got everythin' figgered out right down t' th' end, eh?' he asked.

Nope,' Harris answered evenly. 'Not everythin'.'

'How come? Yuh been dreamin' 'stead o' thinkin'?' Jenkins asked, tauntingly. 'How far didja get? C'mon, speak up. Let's see how a great mind works. It shore oughta be revealin'.'

Harris grinned again.

'Wa-al,' he began, 'furst off, we're headin' fer town.'

'Deadwood?'

Harris nodded briefly.

'Uh-huh.'

'An' then what?' the ranger asked.

'Reckon Carol'd better git thet claim o' hers registered,' Ned continued, ''fore somethin' else happens t' thet map.'

Jenkins considered for a moment.

'Yuh ain't fergot 'bout th' sheriff, hev yuh?' he asked shortly.

'Whut about 'im?'

'Well,' the ranger said thoughtfully, 'what happens when he finds out 'bout th' map bein' lifted offen his deputies? Yuh don' s'pose he's gonna take that sittin' down, do yuh?'

Harris laughed softly.

'Settin' down o' standin' up,' he said. 'It don't make much diff'rence whut he does, once th' claim's been registered.'

The ranger frowned in thought.

'How 'bout them two fellers?' he asked, nodding toward Severs and Willis. 'What yuh aimin' t' do wit' them?'

Ned shrugged his shoulder.

'Nuthin, I reckon,' he replied, "cept turn 'em loose.'

Jenkins considered again.

'S'pose they git t' th' sheriff b'fore we git th' claim registered?' he asked.

Harris grinned fleetingly.

'Then thar'll shore be hell t' pay,' he answered calmly.

'Doggone right there will be,' the ranger said grimly.

Harris looked down at the hard ground for a moment, nudged a rock with his boot toe.

'Mebbe we've wasted too much time already,' he said presently. 'S'pose yuh git goin' now?'

The ranger eyed him sharply.

'Who? Us?'

'Shore,' Harris said quietly. 'You an' th' girl.'

'An' you?' Jenkins demanded. 'What you plannin' t' do?'

'I'm stayin' hyar,' Ned answered calmly. 'I'll give yuh plenty o' time to git t' Deadwood an' register th' claim proper. Then I'll turn them deputies loose.'

Smith Jenkins was silent for a moment. A frown crept over his face. It was obvious that he was weighing the advisability of parting from his long-sought and elusive quarry. Doubts as to the wisdom of such a plan surged into his mind. Still, there was something in the eye of the black-garbed man that quelled his doubts. He looked up again, slowly.

'Yuh aimin' t' foller us t' town?' he asked presently.

Harris nodded without hesitation.

'Soon's I figger th' claim's been 'tended to,' he answered, 'an' it's safe t' let them fellers go, I'll head for Deadwood.'

Jenkins looked at him closely for a moment, then he nodded slowly.

'All right. I'll be lookin' fer yuh,' he said quietly but significantly.

Harris' eyes glinted.

'I'll be thar,' he said curtly.

The ranger shifted his sagging gun belt.

''Jest a minute,' Harris said.

195

'Yeah?'

'Don' let on yuh know me when yuh see me,' he said. 'Savvy? Might be better ef nobody figgered we was both int'rested in this or thet we even knew each other.'

Jenkins nodded.

'Don't s'pose anybody in Deadwood knows yuh or knows thet you're a ranger,' Harris continued. 'Might be a good idea t' keep it quiet. Lotta things yuh might hear an' see'll be covered up ef they fin' out thet you're a lawman. See?'

The ranger nodded again. He turned to Carol.

'Reckon we'll be goin',' he said.

Harris dug into his shirt. He produced the sheet of folded paper that he had found in Severs' pocket.

'S'pose yuh oughta take this 'long wit' yuh,' he said dryly. 'You might need it, y'know.'

Jenkins took the map, shoved it into his pocket. Carol turned slowly and trudged off toward the waiting horses. Jenkins hitched up his belt again and followed at her heels. Harris turned slowly after them. When they neared the horses, the roan looked up, stretched his sleek neck and rubbed his nose against Jenkins' shoulder. The ranger patted his horse's neck, held the stirrup ready, slid Carol's booted foot into it and helped her mount. He caught up the reins in his left hand, gripped the saddle horn with the same hand and swung himself up behind her. Presently, the roan moved off. The big black raised his head and neighed. The roan answered briefly. Jenkins reined in when they came abreast of Harris.

'Be seein' yuh,' the ranger said briefly.

Harris nodded.

'Shore. So long.'

The roan clattered away. Harris turned slowly and looked after them again. He saw Carol turn in the saddle and raise her hand in farewell. He waved his hand in answer. When they were out of sight, he wheeled and trudged away. He halted presently in front of Charley Willis. The deputy looked up.

'Hey, Mister,' he said.

'Yeah?'

'Watcha aimin' t' do wit' us?' Charley asked.

Harris shrugged his shoulder.

'Nuthin', I reckon,' he answered.

Charley sat upright.

'Y' mean yuh gonna turn us loose?' he asked eagerly.

'Shore.'

Willis turned quickly to the prone figure close by.

'Hey, Bill,' he said excitedly. 'Yuh hear

thet?'

The bound figure threshed about for a minute. Severs finally forced himself up into a sitting position. His heavy face was distorted with rage. He glared at Harris.

'Yuh blamed polecat,' he roared. 'Jest lemme git up an' I'll twist yo' neck!'

Harris strolled closer. He halted presently, hooked his thumbs in his belt and grinned down at the struggling Severs.

'Looks like yo' nap didn't do yuh much good,' he said. 'Yo manners an' disposition ain't improved any thet I kin see. Now ef yuh kin shet up an' kinda behave y'self, mebbe I'll jest fergit thet yuh pulled a gun on me an' letcha go.'

Severs scowled darkly.

'I'll hev th' law on yuh fer this, Mister,' he said thickly.

Harris grinned again.

'Thet oughta be easy, bein' thet you fellers are deputies,' he answered.

Severs stared at him for a moment, then he turned furiously upon his companion.

'Why, yuh blamed blabbermouth,' he bellowed. 'I oughta kick yo' teeth down yo' throat!'

Willis paled and pulled away in alarm.

'Now, Bill,' he began hurriedly. 'I didn't tell 'em.'

Severs' thick lips thinned noticeably. His jaws closed with a snap.

''Course not,' he said, then with a flash of scorn in his voice. 'S'pose I tol' im?'

Willis shook his head.

'Heck, no,' he replied. 'He tel' me hisself thet we was deputies.'

Severs glared at him for a moment, then he turned slowly, fixed his eyes firmly upon Harris and looked at him sharply, appraisingly.

'Mister,' he began shortly, 'yuh know a heap more'n yuh oughta. Jest who'n hell are yuh?'

Harris grinned fleetingly.

'Me? Shucks,' he said breezily, 'I'm jest a prospector. I'm allus prospectin', thet is, fer diff'rent things.'

Severs frowned impatiently.

'What's yo' handle?' he asked.

'Marshall,' Ned answered quietly.

'Marshall?' Severs repeated. He frowned again in thought. 'Marshall?' he repeated again, half aloud.

'Mustang Marshall,' Harris said.

Severs' head went up with a jolt. He stared hard at Ned.

'Th' hell yuh are,' he said in a hollow almost awed and incredulous voice.

Harris shrugged his shoulder.

'Suit y'self,' he said, indifferently. 'Yuh asked me, an' I tol' yuh.'

Charley stared at him wide-eyed. He gulped once or twice, swallowed hard and blinked.

'Gosh,' he whispered in awed tones.

Severs gave him a withering glare.

'Shet up,' he said curtly. He studied Harris through half-closed eyes that swept Ned's face, then crept downward over the tall, lithe frame and halted abruptly when they reached the sagging gun belt and the brace of black Colts that swung low against Harris' thighs. 'So you're Marshall, eh?'

Ned made no answer. Steadily he returned the burly deputy's appraising stare. He saw Willis lean over toward his companion, saw his lips move.

'Lookit them eyes,' he heard Willis whisper. 'Jest like they said they was. Like hunks o' ice.'

'We been kinda anxious t' meet up wit' yuh, Mister,' Severs said presently.

Willis nodded vigorously.

'Thet's right,' he said.

Severs turned and glared at him. Charley's eyes faltered. He shifted and looked away. A cold grin swept over Harris' face. It vanished in an instant.

'Oh, yeah? Mebbe yuh ain't been lookin' fer me in th' right places,' he said tauntingly. 'Or

200

mebbe yuh ain't been anxious enuff t' fin' me.'

'I'm givin' it t' yuh straight,' Severs answered quickly. 'Git this rope offen me, willya? Feller cain't talk when he's hogtied.'

Harris grinned again.

''Pears t' me yuh been doin' purty fair so far,' he remarked. He considered for a moment; finally shrugged his shoulder. 'Reckon I might's well untie yuh. Set still fer a minute.'

He bent over Willis and untied the latter's wrists. There was a curious crimson furrow around both wrists, proof of the tautness with which Harris had looped the rope. Charley looked up at him and grinned weakly, massaged his wrists for a minute, stretched himself, then he climbed awkwardly and stiffly to his feet.

'Heck,' he said with a sheepish grin. 'I'm stiffer'n a board from settin' thar.'

Ned worked over Severs' wrists and ankles, then he straightened up, yanked the rope off and tossed it aside. The burly deputy stretched himself, rubbed his cramped legs and wrists, yawned, winced and clamped his jaw shut hurriedly. He put his hand to his jaw and felt it tenderly. Harris watched him quietly. Severs scowled darkly. He opened his mouth to speak, checked himself and shut his mouth again. Ned pretended not to notice.

'Gimme a han',' Severs said gruffly.

'Shore.'

Ned held out his hand. The burly man gripped it and pulled himself up on his feet. Severs stamped his feet for a minute, massaged his arms and wrists again. Harris watched him patiently.

'Now whut was it,' he said presently, 'thet yuh was so anxious t' talk t' me 'bout?'

Severs stopped rubbing his cramped muscles and looked up.

'Huh? Oh, yeah,' he said shortly. 'Look, Marshall, a feller like you oughta go a long ways, providin' o' course, thet yuh got th' right kind o' outfit behin' yuh.'

Ned grinned.

'I been gettin' along purty well by m'self,' he answered.

Severs shook his head impatiently.

'Thet,' he retorted quickly, 'was b'fore they started plasterin' th' country wit' "Wanted" signs 'bout yuh.'

Harris considered for a moment.

'Mebbe,' he answered shortly, begrudgingly.

Severs tapped him on the chest with a stubby, tobacco-stained forefinger.

'Whut a feller like you needs is t' tie up wit' a reg'lar outfit,' he went on earnestly. 'Th'

202

kind thet kin pertect yuh when yuh need it.'

Ned grunted, apparently little impressed.

'Country's full o' tin-horn outfits,' he said
scornfully, 'an' I don't aim t' tie-up wit' none
o' thet kind.'

Severs nodded approvingly.

'Don't blame yuh,' he said. He paused for a
moment. ''Course,' he said slowly, 'they ain't
all like thet.'

'They ain't, huh?' Harris retorted
scornfully. 'I ain't heerd o' none thet ain't.'

Severs smiled craftily.

'I hev,' he said quietly.

Ned's eyebrows arched.

'Yuh kiddin'?' he asked.

The deputy laughed coldly.

'Kiddin', hell,' he said clearly. 'Th' outfit
I'm talkin' 'bout is run by th' two biggest men
in th' West. Does thet sound like a tin-horn
outfit?'

Harris grinned.

'Nope.'

'Yuh wanna hear more?' Severs asked.

'Yuh damn' tootin' I do,' Ned answered
quickly.

The deputy laughed softly.

'Thought thet'd get yuh,' he said presently.
'Th' sheriff runs th' hull county an' Jedge
Parker, wa-al from whut I know o' him, he's
jest 'bout the' biggest and richest man in th'

203

West. Them fellers sound like tin-horns t'
yuh?'

Harris looked sheepish.

'Hell,' he answered. 'How's a feller like me
s'posed t' know there's a outfit like thet doin'
business?'

Severs laughed again.

'Wa-al, yuh know now.'

'I'll say I do.'

The deputy watched him out of the corner
of his eye for a moment.

'Yuh int'rested?' he asked presently.

Harris grinned coolly.

'Whut d' you think?'

Severs turned to Charley Willis.

'Charley,' he said, 'git them things
t'gether.' He nodded towards the pots, cups
and canteen near the flickering fire. 'I'll git th'
horses.'

He turned on his heel and strode away. Ned
looked after him, saw him disappear behind a
distant boulder. He turned slowly and
watched Charley gather up his cooking
utensils. A minute later Severs reappeared,
leading two horses. Charley came forward,
stowed his things away in the spacious saddle-
bags. Severs caught Harris' eye.

'Git yo' horse,' the deputy said briefly.
'We're ridin'.'

Ned nodded, turned and strode over to his

204

horse. The big black looked up. Harris caught up the reins, vaulted into the saddle, wheeled and rode forward. The deputies had mounted and now they clattered off, leaving Harris to bring up the rear. He overtook them presently. Soon the rhythmic echo of the galloping horses faded away in the distance. The flickering camp fire flared up once, then it died out. Minutes later, a huge black bird wheeled high in the sky, circled and swooped down. It swept over the rock-encircled clearing, circled again, dropped lower for a more careful examination of the rope which Harris had tossed away. Barely a foot above it the huge bird swept, screeched angrily in a curiously high-pitched tone, zoomed and winged away again into the limitless sky.

CHAPTER FIFTEEN

When they finally threaded their way out of the hills, Carol relaxed and breathed a deep sigh of relief. Jenkins laughed softly, but inwardly, he too was glad to be on level ground again. He had taken a far different route than Harris had followed in entering the hills, and the last mile had proved to be a hazardous, trail-blazing descent down steep inclines that tested the roan's sure-footedness to the very limit. When they broke into the open, the ranger urged his mount on faster. The roan responded nobly. Presently, his flying hoofs began a drum-roll rhythm that echoed across the vast prairie land.

A heavy pall of dust rose up ahead, billowed high above the trail that led to town. Soon, however, it began to thin out and it dissolved, lifting a veil of obscurity from an approaching stage coach. The four horses pulling it, plunged along the uneven ground and the narrow trail in a wild, careening dash toward the distant town of Cheyenne. There were two men upon the driver's seat; one of them, evidently a guard, looked up quickly when he spied the approaching horse, raised his Winchester in readiness. When the speeding roan came abreast of the stage and Jenkins waved a greeting in passing, the guard relaxed again, lowered his rifle, cradled it in his arms and sank back in his seat. Soon both stage and roan were out of sight of each other.

Soon, too, the ragged hills faded far to the East. Minutes later they saw tiny wisps of smoke climbing skyward, lazily, from a point now not so distant from them. As they sped on, the smoke grew more distinct.

'Reckon thet's Deadwood,' Jenkins said briefly.

Carol made no answer. She raised her head and looked forward with quickening interest. She had never visited Deadwood. She had however heard much about it; heard too of the lawlessness that abounded there. They forded a tiny stream that marked the town's limits, clambered up upon the opposite bank of the stream, and trotted into Deadwood. Carol looked about her interestedly.

Deadwood, she decided at once, was a typical wild-cat town. It had sprung up over night; a jumping-off place for miners and prospectors headed for the hills and the mountains beyond them. With the coming of the miners had come the usual cross-section of life one generally expected to find in a place where the only law the inhabitants knew of was the law of the range, the Colt six-gun and the Winchester. Shacks lined both sides of Deadwood's narrow, muddy street. Some of the shacks were small, others large. The latter were the saloons, the former, the 'respectable' business houses of the town. The former were greatly outnumbered by the latter.

Horses jogged along the muddy street. Men, singly and in groups shouldered their way along the narrow, boarded walks. Here one heard a coarse laugh, a drunken shout, a blow struck, a cry of pain. The latter usually produced a prompt scattering of passers-by,

207

for the blow and the resulting cry were nearly always followed by gun-play. When the latter enactment was concluded and the ensuing smoke of battle had lifted, those who had fled out of gun range, emerged again from their places of safety, glanced fleetingly at whoever had fallen, shook their heads or shrugged their shoulders, or both, and went on their way again. Sometimes a less alert or less nimble-footed passerby was caught between two fires. Often he became the only casualty. The combatants would probably forget their differences, even the blows struck, shake hands, holster their guns and bury the hatchet at the nearest bar. The other passers-by would crowd around the dead man, shake their heads sorrowfully and join in a muttered, 'Pore feller,' and wander away.

One never knew with any degree of certainty just when or where these outbursts would occur. Often, or at least, fairly often, they broke out in the saloons where a heated word, a curse, an implication, could provoke someone less thick-skinned than his mates and result in men backing away from one another, their hands streaking for their Colts. The gun fighters were usually thrown out for the strong-arm men who were employed there to guard against disturbances, had long since learned that property, particularly breakable property, was harder to replace than mere men. The mirrors which adorned the walls of the saloons were costly and highly prized by their owners for it had been necessary to transport them westward from towns hundreds of danger-fraught miles away. Curiously, the mirrors generally suffered the most in indoor gun-fights. Of course, the hugs, hanging lamps that swung from the rafters, suffered too, for often a stray bullet snuffed them out permanently.

The doors of the saloons were usually kept open; in some cases there were no doors at all. It was often necessary to effect an extremely hasty exit and doors simply impeded free movement, that is, to safety. Sometimes, too, a miner who had imbibed too freely, adopted a quaint method of continuing his drinking when his legs began to buckle under him or misbehaved. It was considered good policy to spread one's drinking over as wide an area as possible. Hence, the drinker would manage to get aboard his horse or burro and ride into each saloon and so on until he had visited them all. It was a great help to the drinker for it permitted him to continue his drinking and still motivate without exerting his own fast-failing physical powers of movement.

A man came plunging out of a saloon, sprawled headlong in the muddy street.

Another man followed him, halted in the doorway, spied the sprawled figure, calmly whipped out his gun and fired twice. The sprawled figure lay still. The second man turned. The man lying in the street rolled over. His gun flashed in his hand. He fired twice, one shot flaming hard behind the other. The man in the doorway staggered away, spun on his heel and pitched headlong across the boarded walk. The man in the street arose, holstered his gun, strode over to his fallen adversary, looked at him, gave him a push with his booted foot and rolled him into the street. Then he calmly strode back into the saloon.

Jenkins halted the roan in front of a shack that bore a single-worded, crudely printed sign. It read, 'Sheriff.' He dismounted, helped Carol out of the saddle and nodded briefly toward the shack.

'Reckon thet's th' place,' he said shortly. 'Don't see no other.'

He fell in beside her. They strode across a planked walk. Smith stepped ahead of her, opened the door, held it wide, then followed her inside. He kicked the door shut. A heavy, bearded man was seated behind a small, battered desk, reading a rather mussed newspaper. He looked up slowly when they entered.

'Howdy,' Jenkins said.

The man nodded, looked at him, then at Carol, lingeringly. Jenkins frowned.

'Kin yuh register a claim hyar?' he asked.

The man nodded again. He took his eyes off Carol for a moment and looked up again at the ranger.

'Ef yuh got one t' register,' he said presently. 'What's the name?'

'Register it in th' lady's name,' Jenkins said.

'Shore.'

The bearded man put down his newspaper, opened a drawer in the desk, took out a quill, a bottle of ink, and finally, a small book.

'Whut's th' name?' he asked without looking up.

He thumbed through the book till he found a blank page. Carol looked questioningly at Jenkins. He nodded. She stepped forward to the desk.

'Hall,' she said. 'Carol Hall.'

The man uncorked the bottle of ink, moistened the tip of the quill with his tongue, shifted himself in his chair, then he began to write.

'Whar's th' claim?' he asked presently.

Carol turned to Jenkins who drew the folded sheet from his pocket and handed it to her. Carol took it, unfolded it and handed it to

211

the bearded man. The latter studied it for a moment. The street door opened and two men appeared in the doorway. One was tall and heavy, full faced with quick, shifty eyes. He wore a silver star on his coat lapel. The second man was shorter, slightly built, gray and older than his companion. He was neatly dressed. His face was lined but nicely featured. The bearded man looked up.

'Howdy, Sheriff,' he said quickly. 'Howdy, Jedge.'

The man with the silver star nodded. The 'jedge' smiled.

'How are you, Sam?' he asked.

The sheriff looked at Carol, then at Jenkins, sharply and appraisingly. He strode forward to the desk.

'What's thet?' he asked, nodding toward the map on the desk.

'Thet? Oh, jest a map,' the bearded man answered. 'Regist'rin' a claim for 'er.'

The sheriff held out his hand. Sam handed him the map. The sheriff looked at it, blinked, stared hard at the map, then he wheeled like a flash.

'This yourn?' he demanded of Carol.

'Yes,' she answered quietly. 'It's mine.'

The sheriff scowled darkly.

'Whar'd yuh git it?' he demanded harshly.

Jenkins touched Carol's arm. She turned

212

and looked up at him.

'Reckon th' sheriff ain't uster talkin' t' ladies,' he said quietly.

He motioned for her to step aside. Carol turned away from the desk. She strolled away a bit, halted and turned around again. Jenkins smiled at her, then he turned to the sheriff.

'Ef yuh got any questions t' ask,' he said quietly, 'reckon I kin answer 'em.'

The sheriff glared at him for a moment.

'Who're you?' he demanded.

Jenkins grinned fleetingly.

'Thet ain't important,' he answered. 'Anythin' wrong wit' th' map?'

A frown spread over the sheriff's face.

'I'm sheriff o' this hyar county, Mister,' he said thickly. 'When I asks a question, I wanna answer. Git thet? Whut's yo' name an' whut yuh got t' do wit' this map?'

The ranger turned slightly.

'Carol,' he called.

She came forward again.

'Reckon we come t' th' wrong place,' he said quietly. 'Take yo' map.'

Carol turned to the sheriff and held out her hand.

'Please,' she said quietly.

The sheriff hesitated for a moment. The Colt flashed into Smith Jenkins' hand.

'Han' it over,' he said curtly.

213

The gray-haired man swept past the sheriff. He doffed his hat.

'I beg your pardon,' he said politely. 'I am Judge Parker. Can I be of assistance?'

Jenkins eyed him coldly.

'Dunno,' he answered briefly.

The judge smiled.

'Perhaps if I might be permitted to see the map,' he said. 'I might be able to render you a service.'

Jenkins shrugged his shoulder.

'Go 'head,' he said briefly.

'Thank you,' the judge answered. He turned to the sheriff. 'May I see the map, please?'

Slowly and reluctantly, the sheriff handed it over. The judge took it, looked at it, then he looked up at Carol.

'You claim this map is yours?' he asked shortly.

'I do,' she answered.

'The name written here,' the judge went on, reading from the map, 'is that of one Fred Hall. Do you know such a person?'

Carol smiled.

'Fred Hall,' she answered quickly, 'was my father. I am Carol Hall.'

The judge bowed slightly. He handed her the map.

'Sam,' he said clearly.

'Yeah, Judge?' the bearded man asked.

'Register Miss Hall's claim at once,' the judge ordered. He turned to Carol again. 'You must forgive Sheriff Barton,' he said with a smile. 'The West, you know, is overrun with people of questionable character and sometimes, the sheriff, in his desire to protect our citizens, permits his suspicions to run away with him.'

Carol smiled lightly.

'I understand,' she said briefly.

'How anyone,' the judge continued, smilingly as before, 'could look upon such beauty and still be suspicious, is quite beyond my understanding.' He laughed softly. 'I'm afraid the sheriff isn't as appreciative of beauty as he should be.'

'You flatter me,' Carol answered.

'Not at all,' the judge said gallantly. He turned to the sheriff. 'Come along, Tom.'

The sheriff scowled, stepped past Carol and the judge, gave Jenkins a cold, baleful glare, and strode to the door. He halted there and waited. The judge bowed to Carol.

'Glad to have been of service,' he said with a smile.

He gave Jenkins a brisk nod, turned on his heel, put on his hat and marched to the door. The sheriff threw it open.

'After you, Tom,' they heard the judge say.

The sheriff strode out. The judge followed, closed the door behind him. Jenkins frowned, slid his gun into his holster and strode across the room to the door. He opened it and looked out. After a minute he closed the door, turned slowly and trudged back to Carol's side. She looked up at him questioningly, but he simply shook his head and looked away from her.

Judge Parker and Sheriff Barton walked briskly along the narrow, planked sidewalk. They came abreast of a saloon just as a burly miner, swarthy, dirty and drunk, came staggering out. The man swayed for a moment on unsteady legs, plodded forward and collided heavily with the judge who had circled him in an effort to avoid him.

'Scum,' the judge said coldly and pushed him away.

The miner staggered backward, kept his balance somehow, then he stumbled forward again.

'S'idea shovin' a feller 'roun' like thet, huh?' he said thickly.

'Get out of the way,' the judge said curtly, and pushed him again.

The miner squared off, although he had difficulty keeping himself erect. Another passerby halted for a moment and laughed. The miner whirled, lunged at him, missed and sprawled on his face. The man who had

216

laughed, stepped over him and went into the saloon. The judge and the sheriff continued on their way, turned the corner and strode down a side street and finally entered a narrow doorway. There was no sign above the door, no distinguishing mark to identify it. Up a single flight of stairs they went, halted shortly in front of a closed door at the head of the stairs. The judge produced a key, unlocked the door and threw it open.

It was a small, plainly furnished room that they entered, evidently the judge's office. There was a small desk in the middle of the room, a cabinet in one corner, a crudely-fashioned clothes tree in another. The tree sagged of its own weight against the wall. There were several chairs scattered around the room; one stood behind the desk while still another was placed directly in front. The judge took off his hat, hung it carefully on the tree, turned presently and seated himself behind the desk and finally looked up. Barton halted, shoved the vacant chair out of his way and leaned over the desk. There was a deep frown on his heavy face.

'Now, Parker,' he said thickly, 'mebbe yuh kin tell me whut thet play was all 'bout.'

'You mean about the map?'

The sheriff scowled.

'Yuh know damn' well that's whut I'm

talkin' 'bout,' he growled.

Judge Parker's eyes flashed.

'Don't use that tone with me, Barton,' he said coldly.

Their eyes met and clashed, but in the end it was the sheriff's that faltered and fell beneath the judge's.

'Take off your hat,' Parker said quietly, 'and sit down.'

Barton frowned again. Slowly he removed his hat, glanced at the chair he had shoved away, swung it around again and seated himself.

'That map,' the judge began. 'That was the same one you paid Hawkins to get, wasn't it?'

The sheriff nodded grimly.

'I don't suppose you have any idea as to how the Hall girl regained it, have you?' the judge asked.

Barton shook his head.

'Nope,' he answered sullenly.

'That's what I expected,' the judge said briefly. 'Well, it's all too evident that something went wrong. How and where, I don't know. However, that isn't important. Now, why in Heaven's name did you persist in questioning the girl, once you saw that she had the map? Didn't you realize that you were making them suspicious of you, possibly of me, too?'

The sheriff shifted himself in the chair.

'That's why I had to do something,' the judge went on, 'to cover you up. I wanted to befriend her, to avert suspicion, if possible. Even after it was over, you glared at her and at the young man with her. Barton, you're about as subtle as a bull turned loose in a china shop.'

The sheriff leaned over the desk.

'Yuh tol' me th' mine was wurth aplenty, didn't you?' he demanded.

The judge nodded.

'I did,' he replied briefly.

'Then whut are yuh beefin' 'bout?' the sheriff demanded.

Judge Parker shook his head.

'Your methods, Barton, your methods,' he exclaimed impatiently. 'There are ways of doing things, ways that produce the desired results without having to resort to extremes to obtain them.'

'So now it's my methods, eh?' the sheriff said sneeringly. 'Seems t' me I made yuh a judge usin' th' same methods, didn't I?'

The judge nodded.

'You did,' he answered quietly, 'and I'll never be able to forget it.'

'Wa-al?'

'I'll never be able to forget it,' the judge continued in an even voice, 'because whenever

219

I see you, I realize just how low a man can sink.'

The sheriff bounded to his feet. His face was red with anger.

'Why, yuh dirty hypocrite,' he cried. His hand streaked for his gun.

'Don't touch it,' the judge said quietly.

A small black derringer poked its nose over the edge of the desk. The blunt muzzle pointed directly at Barton's mid-section. Barton saw it, stared hard at it. His hand halted in mid-air. Slowly, he lowered it to the desk. He sat down again, heavily. Presently, the rage left his face.

'Some day, Parker,' he said coldly, 'I'm gonna kill yuh.'

The judge smiled fleetingly.

'No, Barton,' he answered calmly. 'You won't do anything of the kind and you know it. You need me too much. Without me to guide you, they'll hang you higher than a kite.'

The sheriff glared at him, then he dropped back in his chair. The judge pocketed the derringer, then he sat upright.

'Oh, well,' he said presently. 'We're both in this right up to our necks. It's too late to make amends, certainly much too late to start throwing mud at each other. Now we've got to act and act fast if we're to save our precious necks.'

The sheriff turned in his chair.

'Now yuh're talkin' sense,' he said with a grin. 'Whut d' we do?'

The judge frowned momentarily.

'That tall young man with Miss Hall,' he said slowly. 'Sure you've never seen him before?'

The sheriff shook his head.

'Nope.'

'It doesn't matter,' the Judge said. He leaned forward on the desk. 'Tom, this is one thing I've got to entrust you with. Try to do it without being too crude about it.'

It was Barton's turn to frown, and frown he did.

'Huh? Do whut?'

'I'm talkin' about that tall young man,' Parker snapped.

'So I figgered. So whut?'

'If he knows half of what I suspect he knows,' the judge continued, 'we're on our way to the gallows right now. That is, of course, unless...' his voice trailed away.

Barton eyed him sharply.

'Less whut?' he demanded.

Judge Parker's eyes glinted.

'Unless we dispose of him before he can do anything,' he concluded quietly.

The sheriff looked at him for a moment,

curiously.

'Furst time I ever heerd yuh talk like thet, Parker,' he said presently. 'Yuh allus complainin' 'bout me bein' too rough wit' some fellers.' He got to his feet slowly. 'Reckon we kin take keer o' him.'

'He won't be anything like the others,' Parker cautioned.

Barton grinned evilly.

'No?' he drawled. 'Whut makes him so diff'rent?'

The judge smiled fleetingly.

'You'll find out soon enough,' he answered, 'if you miss. He's a ranger, Tom, a ranger.'

The sheriff scowled darkly.

'A ranger, eh?' he repeated. 'So thet's it.'

The judge nodded briefly. Barton kicked his chair out of the way. He clapped his hat on his head.

'I'll git 'im,' he said grimly, 'ef I hafta foller 'im clear t' Hell an' back.'

The door was suddenly flung open. Barton wheeled like a flash. In the doorway stood the 'tall young man.'

'Mebbe I kin' save yuh th' trouble o' makin' thet trip,' they heard Jenkins say.

Sheriff Barton grunted. His hand flashed toward his gun. Jenkins' Colt leaped into his hand. There was a deafening roar, the thunder of blasting guns fired at close range. Smoke filled the room. In the haze a figure coughed, stumbled, fell over a chair and crashed heavily to the floor. The door closed. From the hallway came the sound of a sigh, the sigh of one who is suddenly tired. There was a strange faltering step, then something fell, toppled down the flight of stairs. Presently, everything was still again, the ominous silence that invariably follows an outburst. A slender figure bounded out of the room, fled down the stairs, stepped over a sprawled figure in the narrow doorway and dashed away.

CHAPTER SIXTEEN

Carol Hall sat uneasily at the closed window of her room in Deadwood's only hotel. An hour before, Smith Jenkins had left her there, cautioned her against venturing out and promised to return shortly. She had turned at once to the window. She saw Jenkins enter a saloon across the street then minutes later saw him emerge again, saw him cross back to her side of the street and when he did not appear again, wondered what had become of him. As the minutes flew away, her uneasiness increased. She wished now that Ned Harris would appear. Somehow, his presence seemed to reassure her.

She saw three horsemen wheel into the town's only street. Quickly she raised the window and looked out. Instantly she spied the big black horse and Ned Harris astride him. She breathed a sigh of relief, closed the window and drew her chair closer. She recognized the two men who rode on either side of Harris as the deputies, the burly one as Severs, the other as Willis. She saw them halt in front of the saloon opposite the hotel, saw them dismount and saw them stride inside. She sank down into her chair again.

The three men halted at the bar. The bartender looked up and came forward.

'Howdy, Gents,' he said. 'Whut'll it be?'

The burly Severs scowled.

'Whut d' we look like?' he demanded gruffly.

The bartender grinned a toothless grin.

'Whiskey comin' up,' he droned.

Harris laughed lightly. The bartender slid a bottle of whiskey along the bar. It halted when it collided with Severs' hand. Three glasses followed along the bar. Severs poured himself a stiff drink, put down the bottle, drained his glass and set it down again upon the bar.

'Wait hyar,' he said curtly. 'I'll be back.'

His companions made no answer. The burly deputy turned and strode out. Willis reached for the bottle, poured himself a drink, then he passed the bottle to Harris. The latter filled his glass. Gravely the two men raised their glasses, nodded to each other, drained their glasses and put them down.

'Reckon I'll jest watch them fellers a while,' Willis said, nodding toward the faro table.

'Shore,' Harris answered. 'Go 'head.'

Willis hitched up his belt and strolled away. The bartender removed two of the glasses.

'Travelin' in society, eh, Mister?' he asked.

'Meanin' what?' Harris asked.

The bartender shrugged his shoulder.

'Oh, nuthin' in partic'lar,' he replied. 'Allus strikes me funny when I see a feller keepin' company wit' a coupla deputies.'

Harris grinned fleetingly.

'Oh, yeah?'

The bartender lifted the bottle and wiped the bar.

'Last time I seen yuh, Mister,' he said, 'yuh couldn't rec'llect yo' name,' he said, giving the bar a vigorous wiping.

Harris laughed.

'Funny, how a feller's mem'ry kinda goes back on 'im ev'ry once in a while,' he said.

The bartender nodded.

'Reckon so,' he answered briefly.

Harris leaned over the bar.

'Been hearin' lots 'bout a feller named

Parker,' he said. 'Whar does he hang out?'

The bartender's eyebrows arched.

'Jedge Parker?' he asked.

'Reckon thet's th' feller.'

The bartender wiped the bar again. He kept his eyes averted.

'Lookin' fer 'im?' he asked.

'Some.'

The bartender spied a spot just beyond Harris' elbow. Carefully he wiped it dry.

'They tell me he's plumb deadly wit' a derringer,' he said in a low tone. 'Carries it handy in a shoulder holster.'

'Thet so? Whut else d' they tell yuh?' Harris asked.

The bartender shrugged his shoulder.

'Oh, I dunno,' he answered. He wiped the bar again, vigorously, bent over and examined it critically. 'Thar was 'nother feller in hyar askin' 'bout Parker, too.'

'Tall feller?'

The bartender nodded.

'Light haired?'

'Uh-huh.'

'Sling aroun' his neck?' Harris asked.

'Uh-huh.'

'How long ago?'

'Not long,' came the reply.

'Tell 'im whar t' fin' this Parker?'

The bartender picked up a glass, blew his

breath over it, wiped it clean and held it up. Satisfied with it, he turned and placed it upon a shelf behind him.

'Tol' 'im t' cross th' street,' he said in an undertone, 'then, when he come t' th' corner, t' turn left. Furst door, up one flight.'

Harris hitched up his sagging gun belt, dropped some coins on the bar.

'Reckon I'll go git me some air,' he said briefly.

The bartender nodded.

'Shore.'

'Yuh didn't see me go outta hyar,' Harris said quietly.

'Nope,' came the brief reply.

Harris turned and strode out. Carol, still seated at her window, saw him cross the street, then he disappeared. She waited, expecting to see him reappear but after a few minutes, she sank back in her chair.

Harris strode briskly along the sidewalk. When he reached the corner, he turned into the side street. At the first door, he turned in. He tripped over something in the doorway, caught himself and looked down. A frown spread over his face. Smith Jenkins lay at his feet. Swiftly he bent over the ranger.

'Jenkins,' he said.

The ranger stirred. Slowly he opened his eyes, looked up at Harris and managed a weak

227

grin.

'Yuh hit bad?' Harris asked.

'Dunno,' came the whispered answer. 'Jest kinda tired an' sleepy.'

'Whut happened?' Harris demanded.

'Parker an' Barton,' Jenkins whispered. 'Upstairs.'

'Who's Barton?'

'Jenkins moistened his lips with his tongue.

'Sheriff,' he whispered. 'He got me.'

'An' Parker?'

Jenkins shook his head.

'Dunno. Rec'nized him. He owned th' bank. Made dad git ranchers t' borrer frum th' bank. Made 'em sign duplicate papers. Took their ranches from 'em,' he mumbled wearily. He closed his eyes for a moment, then slowly reopened them. 'Tol' yuh dad didn't steal yo' father's ranch. 'Member?'

Jenkins closed his eyes again. Harris stepped into the street again. He spied two men across the street.

'Hey,' he called.

The men halted and looked over at him.

'C'mere, willya?' he called.

Quickly the men strode across.

'Wa-al?' one of them asked.

'Got a doctor in this hyar town?' Harris asked.

The man nodded quickly.

'Shore. Right 'cross th' street,' he answered.

Harris led them into the doorway.

'Carry this feller over thar, willya?' he asked.

The man eyed him curiously.

'You plug 'im?' he asked.

Harris' eyes glinted.

'Nope,' he answered curtly. 'I'm gonna git th' feller that did. Y'know Jedge Parker?'

The man's eyes opened wide.

'Parker do thet?' he asked.

'I didn't say he did, did I?' Harris retorted. 'Jest tell me whut this Parker feller looks like.'

'Oh,' the man began, 'he's kinda little. Kinda sporty feller, too. Allus spruced up. Got gray hair. I reckon yuh'll know 'im th' minute yuh see 'im.'

Harris nodded briefly.

'Reckon I will,' he answered. 'Now willya do like I said?'

The men bent over Jenkins.

'An' tell th' Doc,' Harris said quickly, 'thet I'll be 'long directly, jet soon's I 'tend t' some other bus'ness.'

The men lifted the unconscious Jenkins. Harris saw them carry him across the street to the doctor's house, saw the door open, saw them disappear inside. Grimly he hitched up his belt, then lightly he raced upstairs. At the

229

head of the stairs he halted, spied a slightly opened door, crept forward and looked into the room.

A chair lay on the floor and just beyond it, the outstretched body of a big man. Ned stepped inside. He turned the man over. He saw at a glance that the man was dead.

'Reckon thet's one for you, Jenkins,' he said half aloud.

Then he noticed the silver star on the dead man's shirt front.

'So you're Barton, eh?' he mused.

He glanced around the room, spied the cabinet in the corner of the room, and strode over to it. He ripped open the cabinet doors and looked inside. When he was satisfied that no one was hiding in it, he slammed the doors, strode out of the room and raced downstairs. In the doorway he halted and pondered a moment.

Severs, he recalled, had dashed off without mentioning where he was going. Willis, he recalled too, had made no protest nor had he suggested accompanying him. The chances were, Ned decided, that Severs had gone to the sheriff's office to report. Perhaps Parker had gone there too. Harris stepped out of the doorway, strode briskly down the street. He plunged around the corner, came to an abrupt halt and flattened out against the side of a building when he saw two men trudge across the muddy street and enter the saloon he had left. One of the men was Severs. His companion was slight and neatly dressed. Harris' eyes glinted dangerously. He dashed across the street.

From her window, Carol saw him approach the saloon. She got to her feet quickly. He hesitated about entering, then he seemed to glide inside. Something in his manner stirred her. She saw him halt in the doorway, saw his hands drop to the butts of his guns. She turned away from the window, flew out of the room and raced down the hallway. At the head of the stairs she collided with a berouged, hard-faced woman in an abbreviated costume. Carol drew back when the woman gave her an icy stare. Hands on hips, the woman blocked the way.

'What's the rush?' she asked coldly. 'Goin' to a fire?'

She straightened her costume, smoothed her hair with a slim white hand. Carol murmured an apology, stepped around her and fled down the stairs. The corridor of the hotel was filled with tobacco smoke and men; big, rough, coarse-looking men who looked up with interest when she appeared, halted their conversation and eyed her covetously. A man lounging in the doorway looked up too when she approached, smiled and took a step forward in her direction.

'Why, hello, honey,' he said.

Carol tried to get past him, but he put out his hand and caught her by the arm.

'Whut's th' hurry?' he asked.

She broke away from him, struck him across the mouth with her open hand and fled into the street.

The man wheeled.

'Yuh damn' hell-cat,' he snarled. He put his hand to his bruised lips and cursed her.

She hesitated for a brief moment at the sight of the thick, soft mud in the gutter, then she dashed across. Midway she narrowly avoided colliding with a man who was crossing from the opposite side of the street, bent under the weight of a huge box. Two horsemen jogged by, reined in to allow her to pass. One of the men leaned down over the side of his horse and said something to her, but Carol slipped past him. His companion laughed. The first man looked after her, scowled, then he spurred his horse and went on.

She halted just outside the saloon door, moved aside quickly when two men brushed past her and strode inside to the bar. She turned to a window and looked in. Just inside the saloon, abreast of the bar, stood Harris. He had halted there. He seemed to be looking for someone. Slowly, he began to advance. Men looked up at him from their tables. Some of them, glimpsing his grim face, sensed trouble and arose hastily and drifted away. Presently she saw Harris halt again. She followed his eyes.

At a corner table sat three men. Two of the men were deputies. The third man, she noted at once, was Judge Parker. She turned away from the window and stepped inside the open doorway. The babble of voices she had heard before seemed strangely hushed now. She heard chairs scrape on the wooden floor, heard someone cough.

The three men at the corner table turned slightly as Harris looked at them. The judge's face was ashen and streaked.

'I've come fer yuh, Parker,' she heard a hard, cold voice say. She recognized it with a start as Harris.

Men melted away, scampering quickly out of range.

'Willis,' she heard Ned say presently. The deputy looked up slowly. He gulped audibly. 'Git up outta that.'

'Yuh-yuh want me?' he stammered. 'I—I ain't done nuthin' t' nobody.'

'Git up,' Harris repeated curtly.

Slowly the man climbed to his feet. He leaned against the table for support.

'Face th' wall,' Harris ordered briefly.

Willis shrugged his shoulder, turned slowly and faced the wall.

'Severs,' Ned said dully.

The burly deputy scowled darkly.

'What d' yuh want?' he demanded.

'Git up,' came the answer.

Slowly and reluctantly, Severs arose.

'Buckin' the law, Mister,' he said thickly, 'ain't gonna git yuh no place.'

Carol heard Ned laugh scornfully.

'Law?' he repeated. 'Whut law? Th' law thet pertects hellions like him?' nodding toward the silent Parker.

Severs made a move. A Colt flashed into Harris' right hand. Severs merely grunted and hitched up his belt. Harris grinned fleetingly.

'Face th' wall,' he commanded, 'an' raise yo' han's.'

The burly deputy scowled again, turned toward the wall and slowly raised his hands. The crowd leaned forward now for as everyone knew, Parker would be called upon next.

'Parker,' they heard Harris call curtly.

There was a general craning of necks. Here some of the crowd climbed upon their chairs to watch Parker answer the summons. Slowly, almost mechanically, he started to rise. Suddenly his right hand streaked inside his

234

coat. Flame spurted from his shoulder. Harris' heavy Colt thundered in protest. The judge sagged forward against the table, then slowly he forced himself up. His right hand hung limply, shattered and useless. While all eyes watched, he shifted a small, black derringer to his left hand. He looked up suddenly and fired again. The Colt answered. Smoke swirled around Harris. The derringer fell to the floor.

Again the judge forced himself up. He came around the table, halted in front of it, both arms hanging limply now. He seemed strangely bent, barely able to keep his feet. Blood surged down one hand and dripped gently to the floor. He braced himself against the table and looked up, a curious, defiant smile on his ashen face. Calmly he waited. Then the Colt roared again, once, twice, three times more. Judge Parker swayed, spun and pitched forward on his face. No one moved. Smoke curled ceilingward from Harris' gun. Slowly he shoved it back into its holster, turned abruptly and strode toward the door. As Ned came abreast of him, the bartender caught his eye and nodded. Harris acknowledged it with a nod of his own.

He quickened his pace when he saw a slim, white-faced girl awaiting him in the open doorway. He came swiftly to her side. Her

235

anxious eyes swept his face.

'Yuh shouldn'ta come hyar,' he said gently but reproachfully.

'I had to, Ned,' she answered in a small voice. 'I saw you go in there, alone. Nothing mattered after that 'til I saw you turn and come toward me. Then I knew what I should have realized was true that first night in the hills. I know now, Ned, that I loved you even then.'

She took his arm, held it tightly, proudly and possessively. He smiled down at her, then slowly they trudged out. Passers-by who had gathered around the door, gave way before them. Among those who stepped back was a man with bruised lips. Carol saw him standing there. The man paled, turned and strode away.

It was evening again and now the bright moon flooded the valley with yellow light. A cool breeze swept down from the cliffs and sifted through the brush, whipped noisily through the branches of the tall trees. Presently, it died down. The brush was still, dripping with shadows, while the far-flung branches of the tall trees drooped silently almost mournfully. In front of the house, the big black horse pawed the ground impatiently, anxious to be off. Perhaps he sensed that a long trip lay ahead of him, for hanging from the saddle were bulky and freshly-filled saddle bags. Then too there was a new blanket roll behind the saddle. Even the Winchester in the saddle boot had been cleaned and reloaded in preparation for the long journey.

A slim girl and a tall man stood together in the shadows just beyond the horse. In a few minutes Ned Harris would be gone. The girl clung to him. They had said their goodbyes many times in the past half hour, still there was always another to be said. She clung to him, pleaded with him to take her along with him. Always he refused.

'It ain't right,' she heard him say over and over again. 'You're purty an' young an' educated. I ain't none o' them things, 'cept mebbe that I ain't so much older'n yuh. Still, I been a marked man. Thar's things I gotta live down, fergit an' start over wit'.'

Just as often she had countered with:

'But those things belong to another day, Ned, when you weren't Ned Harris but "Mustang" Marshall. I saw that other man, that Marshall, saw him and feared him. He's gone out of your life. Now you're just Ned Harris. Those things Marshall did, died when he died.

'The first time I saw you, Ned, you seemed so cold, so hard, so merciless. Oh, Ned, you

237

aren't any of those things. I couldn't love you if you were. It isn't because I love you or that I'll marry you in a minute, or that I'll gladly go to the end of the earth with you if that's where you want to go, that I say this. You've been a victim of circumstances, and each act of reprisal on your part has led the authorities to charge you with still another crime.'

Everything else had entered into their conversation, and now they were finished with them. Redburn, the mining engineer, had looked over Carol's property, pronounced it extremely valuable and had offered to work it for her on a percentage basis. Ann and he would be married. The three of them would make their home in Carol's old home.

As for Smith Jenkins, he had suffered a wound in his side. Finding it more painful than serious, the town doctor had granted them permission to move the wounded man down into the valley. He had also consented to accompany his patient and spend a few days there. Now Jenkins lay in Ned's own bed, frowning up at the ceiling above him. When Ann looked in, he managed a grin and asked to see Ned before he left. He wasn't finished with him yet.

Harris was still proving a stubborn individual. California, he stoutly maintained, was too far away. He wouldn't even consider asking or allowing her to make such a long and perilous journey, even if he wanted to take her along.

Ann came striding down the path from the house. They turned slowly as she drew near.

'Ned,' she said quietly. 'Jenkins is awake and asking for you. Will you see him, please, before you go?'

'Shore,' he answered quickly. 'I'll see 'im now.'

He stepped past Carol, strode up the path and into the house. Ann and Carol faced each other in the moonlight.

'He's going,' Carol said in a dull voice.

'Yes,' Ann answered gently, 'I know.'

'I'll never see him again,' Carol said wretchedly.

Ann came closer. She took Carol's hand in hers.

'If you love him, Carol,' she said quietly, 'let him go.'

Carol looked up sharply.

'Let him go?' she repeated.

Ann nodded.

'Yes,' she went on. 'Give him a chance to find himself, alone, to adjust himself to the new life he'll find there. Then, if you still want him, go to him.'

They heard Ned's quick step to the path. Together they turned to face him. He halted in front of them.

'Reckon Jenkins is gonna be fine,' he said presently. 'Complainin' a'ready 'bout bein' cooped up in the house,' he laughed softly. 'Funny, ain't it,' he mused, 'how things work out? Coupla days ago I wouldn'ta believed it, but hyar I am, likin' th' feller.'

There was an awkward silence after that. He looked down at them, studying them so intently as though he were making a mental picture of each, then bent slowly and kissed Ann's cheek. She put her hand quickly to her mouth to stifle the sob that rose in her throat and fled up the path and into the house. Harris took Carol's hands in his.

'Adios,' he said gently.

'Adios,' she answered quietly.

Gently he released her hands, turned toward the horse, halted, and wheeled again to face her. For a brief moment they stood there, looking at each other, then with great suddenness she was in his arms and he was crushing her to him. She clung to him, raised her head and gave him her lips. Presently, he released her, turned again and vaulted into the saddle. The big black wheeled, then they clattered away into the night.

Minutes later she heard a hail from the cliff and looked up quickly. They had halted there for a last goodbye, a black figure on a great black horse. For a moment they stood out boldly, silhouetted against the sky, then horse and rider took the westward trail. Slowly, heavily, Carol turned, trudged up the path and into the house.

Photoset, printed and bound in Great Britain by
REDWOOD BURN LIMITED, Trowbridge, Wiltshire